I0647463

Sex, Stories and Power Exchange

Adventures – And Lessons –
Of a Naughty Power Exchange Couple

First Edition

The Nazca Plains Corporation
Las Vegas, Nevada
2011

ISBN: 978-1-61098-243-6
E-Book: 978-1-61098-244-3

Published by

The Nazca Plains Corporation ®
4640 Paradise Rd, Suite 141
Las Vegas NV 89109-8000

PUBLISHER'S NOTE
Sex, Stories and Power Exchange – Adventures – And Lessons – Of a Naughty Power Exchange Couple is partially a work of fiction created wholly by *Dan and Dawn Williams* imagination. All characters are fictional and any resemblance to any persons living or deceased is purely by accident. No portion of this book reflects any real person or events.

Cover Photo, William Langeveld
Art Director, Blake Stephens

DEDICATION

Our thanks to the many people who helped us on this journey, both directly and indirectly. Be it that you are one of the co-stars of one of these stories (names changed to protect the naughty) or someone who helped us work out feelings of jealousy or concern, we appreciate the many friends and lovers who helped us along the way.

Warmest regards,

Dan and dawn Williams, 2011

Sex, Stories and Power Exchange

Adventures – And Lessons –
Of a Naughty Power Exchange Couple

First Edition

Dan and Dawn Williams

INTRODUCTION

Is this book fiction? Nonfiction?
Self help? Porn? A love story?

Yep. And you'll be, I am afraid to say, hopelessly lost (but very turned on) if you skip this introductory part. Like some other couples, Dan and dawn whispered naughty stories to each other while in the bedroom and sometimes actually took the step to write them down. After some time went by, dawn looked up at Dan from the middle of a very naughty sex scene they were having and said, "Didn't we write this as a story of something we wanted to do one day?" They sat back, realizing that this was indeed the case, and reflected on all the work they had done and what it took to get there (and that they had some stories that were still only stories) and this book was born. Thus, you have in your hands our adventures, things we've learned along the way, and some fantasies that have yet taken breath.

ABOUT THE STORIES

There are ten erotic stories throughout the book. Of those, nine have 'made up' names in them. Six of them are their past – these are the things Dan and dawn have done. Although the names have been changed to protect the naughty, the stories are adventures they have experienced, enjoyed, and learned from. Four of them are not yet (or maybe will stay forever fantasies). We leave it to the reader to figure out which are which. One story even uses their names, but is it really about them? Hmmmmmmm....As you read the segues, you'll get to know Dan and dawn. And that will assist you perhaps in deciding which of these are things they would do… and which they'd only do in stories.

ABOUT HOW THE SEGUES
WERE WRITTEN

As you read segues, you'll notice certain sections are annotated with "Dan says" and other sections "dawn says". We did not do this to confuse our readers, promise. But this is indeed a joint effort by a pair of people who are husband and wife, erotic dominant and slut, paired in a power exchange relationship, friends, and in this, co-authors. The book reflects not only their joint view, but their individual perspectives as well as their own experiences. If you have heard them present or lead a workshop, or heard them co-host their internet radio show, "Erotic Awakening", you'll be reminded of that same style – as if you are sitting with them as they speak in the way that is natural to them.

You'll notice right off the bat one thing that people will find either odd, annoying, or perfectly normal. We will refer to dawn with a lower case "d", and to Dan with an upper case "D". Sometimes, dawn will use a lower case 'i' as well, to refer to herself. We hope that if this seems strange and gives you a grammar migraine that you will allow us this leeway – it works in our life and perhaps you'll see some value in it. Or you'll just let it go.

FOREWORD

The line between fantasy and reality is often a very harshly delineated boundary in many people's minds (and in their intimate relationships). Our western culture tells us that our sexual behavior should fit into one of a few boxes – married and monogamous, chaste dating, and so on – but rarely do we get the permission to express the fantasies that drive our desires. Even more rarely do we find that we can have those fantasies and still have the kind of relationships that we want to have...so most of us go through our lives feeling bad that we have the desires we do, and putting up barriers between our lovers and ourselves because we never have the guts to talk about it with them.

In this book, Dan and dawn happily bend that line, blur it, move it aside, and even erase it – and talk about how and why they do it. From the scorching sexiness of the stories they weave, to the practical (and utterly honest) stories of their own experiences coming to terms with sluthood, they will guide you through the process of considering your own fantasies, talking about them, and perhaps even living a few of them out. They cover both the responsibility – the trust, the safe words, the negotiation – as well as the intimacy and joy of exploring fantasies both in the bedroom and beyond.

Of course, if you just want some hot and heavy one-handed reading…you'll get that, too. The first story leads you through a woman's desire to please her master while living out her fantasy of finding (and being dominated) by a stranger online. Subsequent stories explore the delicious experience of being dominated by a group of people, the edgy sensuality of exhibitionism, the ecstasy of sacred sex, and beyond. Each story brings forth images to our minds eyes, and (in my case, at least) spur my own thoughts, fantasies, and memories.

Use this book as a way to talk with your partner about your fantasies, and theirs. Let it guide you by example, as a mentor or trusted friend would. Let it give you glimpses of your own sexuality, at its best and most pleasurable. And most of all, let it inspire you to take a risk to trust, to explore, and to bring about a level of love and intimacy to your life that you've always desired.

With lust in my heart,

Sarah Sloane
2011

LET THE ADVENTURE BEGIN

CONTENTS

HOTEL SPANKING

"You won't cum again until you find a man to play with."

Lynn had never had this kind of command from her master before. She'd been with many other men at his direction, but he'd always been the one to set things up. Now, apparently, it was time for her to learn, and her pussy clenched every time she thought about it as the need to cum merged with the intense desire to please the man who owned her.

How does a slut hunt for a man? Lynn had put a lot of thought into the question in the days after her task was given. She lurked around online chat groups at first, driving herself almost mad with fantasies as she watched the letters flow by on the screen, messages of lust and explicit promise, typed by unseen hands. At first she was entranced by the idea that any of those hands might belong to him, the one man she was looking for. Her nipples would tighten as they flirted, words entwining with ideas that made her breath catch at the images they inspired. Time after time she was frustrated as the internet liaisons failed to develop into anything more concrete, and she was left their hands shaking over her keyboard, pussy drenched, clit throbbing, with no release.

You won't cum again until you find a man to play with.

As the days passed, she became more brazen. Her typing became faster, more curt, flowery descriptions abandoned in favor of blatant propositions. Here I am. Use me. Her words became a blunt instrument, like the kind she wanted to use in her pussy. She couldn't – she could only clench her fists uselessly against her thighs, her obedience to her master absolute and torturous. There were nights when her entire body shook with the arousal of talking sex with so many other lascivious minds, but she didn't dare even stroke between her legs. Master had said: you won't cum again until…

One of her aliases was for a spanking group, and for a change her Looking to play IRL message finally seemed to intrigue the right kind of person. His user name (use her, yes, use me! she thought) was HardJim, and the implications of the simple adjective appealed to her. Hard man. Hard cock. Hard spanking. Like her, he didn't seem to be as interested in weaving elaborate fantasies as he was in real-life action. After a few messages she got his picture, and sent her own…and suddenly maybe turned into right now. HardJim wanted her that evening.

Lynn felt a different kind of tension inside of her as she printed out the email and chat logs and went to kneel before her master, presenting it for his review. He read their exchange silently, as she knelt, hoping the man would be acceptable. His expression didn't change as he looked up from the paper – alert, watchful, measuring. "Is he the one?" he asked, simply.

"I hope so, Master. I…I think so. Please, may I try, Sir?"

Something of the pent-up desire must have leaked into her tone and pleased him. An amused and loving smile brightened his face. "Then make it happen, slut, and we'll go see him tonight."

Lynn managed not to quite run back to the computer, eager to email HardJim her cell number. A moment later it buzzed, and she almost came on the spot just from anticipation.

"Is this Lynn?" came his voice over the line. It was a friendly baritone, and Lynn imagined he would have a nice laugh.

"Yes...is this...HardJim?" she felt suddenly like a high schooler, shaky with anticipation.

He laughed, and it was nice. "Just Jim is fine. I was thinking of a hotel..." Quickly he described the place to meet, sounding almost as eager (if not as desperate) as she was.

The hotel was a half-hour away, and she gave a quick description of her Master and what she'd be wearing. "No," came his unexpected but firm reply.

"Excuse me?" she stammered, for a moment thinking the rug would be pulled out from under her. "But...I told you from the start, Master needs to be there – "

"Of course he does," Jim said, voice still even. "I'm quite looking forward to meeting him. But you'll wear what I want you to – and that's a nothing but a sundress. No panties." Lynn felt her pussy swell at the confident demand in his tone. "But you should bring a little toy bag with you. Just a few of your favorite things." He paused, waiting for her to reply, but she couldn't think of what to say, just giving a tiny mmm of assent. "Good. I'll look forward to seeing you, Lynn." He closed the call before she could respond.

It took a moment of standing there, the thought of It's really going to happen! running through her mind, before she was able to make her feet take her to the bedroom. The sundress was easy to choose, a lovely sea-green pattern with soft pastel white and yellow highlights. It came down just below her ass, too, and in a strong wind everyone would see...she shivered and put that particular fantasy away, continuing to pack for her assignation.

What to bring? She looked over her master's collection of implements with an experienced eye, knowing intimately how everything would feel against the tender skin of her ass. This was not punishment, this was play, so no need to go overboard – her lips pursed as she selected the items for her erotic spanking date. Leather paddle. Leather strap (her arm got goosebumps as she picked it up, feeling the weight, remembering the orgasmic tears it had brought her). A ping-pong paddle, because this was play, after all, and also the wooden hairbrush because sometimes the classics were just too good to pass up.

After a moment she also grabbed some condoms, a few packets of lube, and her favorite vibrator. Hope sprang eternal, and this was fulfilling her Master's directive. If this man's erotic spanking happened to include fucking her until she came, who was she to argue?

Even as she packed them in the bag, though, her mouth curled in a wry smile. Her Master never made things that easy – that was part of why she loved him. Cumming wasn't important. Pleasing him was everything.

She was almost bouncing as they drove to the hotel, nervous excitement building with every mile. Master's hand on her bare leg felt like a direct line to her wet pussy, and she realized if he simply commanded her she could cum on the spot. This is happening, this is really happening she thought over and over, trying to convince herself. As her master looks over at her with a sparkle in his eye, Lynn realized she had been saying it out loud, under her breath. Embarrassed, she grinned at him, saucy but servile. As they pulled into the parking lot, she whispered in his ear. "Thank you, Sir."

Jim stood next to his red sports car, waiting for them. He looked to be in his mid-40's, with a handsome face and short brown hair. His golf shirt and slacks fit well, and the easy smile he gave as they pulled up next to his car made Lynn relax a tiny bit. Not only was this happening, but it was going to be good.

She was about to get out of the car, but Master's hand tightened on her leg. "Wait here," he ordered, and got out to meet

Jim. She watched them talking, suddenly feeling anxious again. They didn't seem to be arguing, but her Master was looking at her, then back to Jim, then back to her in the car. Lynn felt the doubt start to creep in. What if her Master didn't like Jim? What if she'd missed something about him that made him unsuitable? What if Master didn't let her play?

You won't cum until…

Her fears suddenly were interrupted by a rap on the window, and startled, she looked up to see Jim smiling down at her, outside the car. She'd been so caught up that she hadn't even seen them approach, and she hurriedly pressed the button to roll down the window.

"Hey, Lynn," Jim said. "You still up for this?" At her eager, smiling nod, his grin widened. "OK, then. I'm going in to get a hotel room. I'll call your cell phone and let you two know which room." He walked into the hotel as her Master opened the door for her and motioned for her to get out.

She looked at him, feeling a little shy. "Is he…ok, Sir?" she asked.

Master laughed and opened his arms to enfold her in a hug. "He's fine, little one. You did a very good job at finding someone who seems to know what he's doing. Well done, girl," he squeezed her harder. "I'm proud of you," he whispered in her ear, and she knew that nothing that came after that would feel as good as those simple words from his lips.

She luxuriated in his embrace for a timeless moment, but her cell phone buzzed and interrupted her reverie. She looked up at her Master. "Room 23," she said, suddenly feeling breathless and shy, and her legs felt weak as he motioned her to walk into the hotel. He took her hand and led her, giving her strength.

Far sooner than she expected they were standing outside of Jim's hotel room, and

Master indicated that she should knock. It took Lynn three tries to make a real noise against the door, and her shyness exploded as the door began to open. She actually took a step back, wanting to cower and hide behind her master, but before she could he pushed her roughly into the room.

"Put the toybag on the dresser and attend me," her Master ordered, moving to sit on the small couch. Jim sat on the edge of the bed, facing him, and a moment later Lynn knelt gracefully at her Master's feet. Her knees were open, hands on her thighs, and her head tilted slightly forward as Master's hand twined in her hair. A peace came over her at this familiar place, and her shyness vanished, replaced by a steadily increasing burn of desire.

"Mmm," Jim said, appreciatively. "Always nice to see dominance and submission done right."

Master nodded, accepting the compliment. "She takes to it well."

"Nice. How does she want to be spanked?" Lynn felt a thrill at the simple act of being omitted from the conversation; she belonged to Master, and was his to decide how best to be used.

"Erotic, as she requested," he said, and she felt her pussy throb. "And hard." His voice deepened almost to a growl as he said that, and it seemed to reverberate through her even as his fingers tightened in her hair. "I want to see her hot and squirming under your hand or the paddle." He paused, then his hand released her, waving in dismissal.

"Beyond that, you can pretty much do what you want. I'll just be over here, out of the way. If you fuck her mouth or pussy, wear a condom, that's the only rule. You can cum in her, or take the condom off and cum on her." Lynn could hardly believe the cavalier way her master talked about her, or how much it was exciting her. "Oh, by the way, Jim.

She's a painslut. Don't worry about going too hard or too much with the paddle. And don't worry about making her cum. That doesn't matter – she just wants to get you off, to have you enjoy what she's offering. Isn't that right, Lynn?"

Lynn looked up then, eyes wide and shining with devotion. "Yes, Master," she said, clearly and simply.

"Show Jim the toys you brought to play with," Master ordered with a smile.

Lynn rose gracefully form her knees, then her eagerness overcame her composure and she bounced over to the bag, tearing the zipper open and laying out the paddles, strap, and comically large blue vibrator on the bed. Her hand lingered on it for a moment, hoping that Jim would catch the hint but afraid to look up. "Lynn !" her master's voice cut through her fantasy, and she obediently moves quickly to kneel again at his feet. Her breath was coming fast and hard, and she tried vainly to calm it, to steady her thoughts.

Master let her sit there a moment, then he started things off with a command. "Go. Ask him to spank you."

Taking one more deep breath, she stood, not so gracefully this time – her legs felt shaky again. She bowed her head and moved towards the man who would spank her ass – and perhaps more – that evening. Jim sat calmly at the edge of the bed, waiting patiently for her, letting the locus of control smoothly move from her Master to him as her playmate for the evening. As she stood in front of him, she couldn't quite bring herself to look up into his eyes, but her voice was clear. "Jim, sir, will you spank me?" Another deep breath, and then she added, in a smaller voice, "Please?"

Jim took her hand, moving her closer, directly in front of him, and then took the hem of her sundress between his fingers. Lifting it slowly, he watched her face change, the emotions flickering around and around. Fear, lust, desire, shyness, anxiety, wanton sex…her mouth opened slightly as she began to be overcome with the moment, and he used his other hand to touch her between her thighs, fingers pressing firm just for an instant on her mons just over her clit. Her mouth opened wider then, and he slid his fingers down, slipping into the warm wet cleft that is drenched with the juices flowing from her engorged pussy.

Before she could do so much as thrust her hips he withdrew the fingers, leaving her wanting and breathing harder through her parted lips. "Turn around. Show me your ass." Wordlessly she obeyed his command, lifting her dress for him and pushing her ass out with a small curve of her lower back, just the way her master had taught her.

Jim reached up and squeezed her cheeks hard enough to be just short of pain, and Lynn gasped. When he let go he followed up with two strikes, sharp slaps on each cheek, and she let out a soft cry. It's beginning, she thought, reaching out to grab the dresser and push her ass out further. When Jim didn't continue, she moaned softly, her ass moving slightly side to side, as if seeking out the hand to abuse it.

"Stand up," he says curtly, and at the sharp tone she straightened, conditioned to obey.

"Lay across my lap," he ordered her, and she turned to see him sitting on the corner of the bed. A moment later she was in that humiliating and familiar place, stretched over his knees, feeling him lift her dress, a cool draft of air caressing her throbbing wet cunt.

As he began to spank her, Lynn's body relaxed and she groaned with the joy of every impact as it drove through her body directly to her core.

Jim lived up to his name, spanking her hard and fast, the harsh smacks coming quick and without hesitation. There was no warmup, this was simply brute force on willing flesh, and Lynn let herself fall into the sensation. Suddenly he pushed two fingers deep into her willing cunt, his thumb stroking her clit, fingers thrusting, pinching, pulling as she writhed on his lap.

She felt naughty, a willful slut put in her place and given what she deserved, what she wanted oh, so badly. Given to a stranger, laying wanton over his lap as he spanked her bare ass and finger-fucked her pussy. Lynn squirmed and moaned into the bedspread, clenched tight in her fists as Jim, Hard Jim, slammed his open palm against her ass again and again, only stopping long enough to drive his fingers maddeningly into her, teasing. She could feel her juices begin to cover her ass, making his hand sting her skin even more, and the added pain only made her more wet. She moaned again, trying to keep enough presence of mind to remember they were in a hotel and walls were thin.

But it was hard, because Jim was so good at this, and this was what she wanted, what she needed.

She heard someone begging "Let me take it off! Please let me be naked for you! Please, use my tits, my nipples, please!" and only gradually realized it was her voice after he granted permission, pushing her up. Her head felt muzzy and her ears roared with the rush of blood and her pounding heart. Jim just watched, along with her Master on the couch, as she struggled out of it, exposing her breasts heaving with shallow breaths to their gaze and his touch.

As she stood, naked, wondering what he was going to do to them, he shook his head.

"Not done yet," Jim muttered, and grabbed her by the back of the neck, pushing her face down onto the coverlet. He lightly kicked her feet to a wider stance on the floor, so that her ass was high in the air, pussy open to him, her cheeks red and pulsing in time with her heartbeat. Lynn held that pose as Jim walked to the dresser, and she knew he was going to come back with one of her toys. She flexed her legs slightly, moving up on the toes, feeling the wonderful vulnerability and the sweet burn of her skin from his hands.

Suddenly he was next to her again and she felt the harsh whack of the hairbrush against her ass. Lynn gasped aloud at the impact and the intense heat that followed as the nerves fired in sympathetic reaction. Her legs spread wider, pussy begging for more, even as her feet tried to move away, to crawl onto the bed to escape the inexorable pain as he struck again. Jim lay his free hand against the base of her spine and she felt a strange stillness come over her. Her ass was still on fire, but somehow her mind divorced from the fear or any thought of escape. This was where she belonged, this was where she wanted to be, and her pussy wanted to be here most of all.

This feeling was amplified as Jim suddenly shoved the beautiful blue vibrator between the lust-slick lips of her pussy. With no subtlety he cranked it on high and she let out a wordless sound of need, grinding back against it even as the hairbrush smacked again, harder, and again. She wriggled and trembled in succession, the pain and pleasure filling her mind with a white-hot light.

Jim selected the leather paddle next, raining down strikes on her upper thighs while he fucked her hard and deep with the vibrator. The sharp staccato of the paddle on her flesh is in counterpoint to the liquid sounds of his hand gripping the vibe and pushing in and out of her sopping cunt, and it is the only sound beyond her hoarse breath in the room. The sensations layered over each other, coming apart and merging again in overlapping waves. Each throbbing second thrust her blow by blow towards an explosion that always seemed just a bit too far out of reach – but there was no going back.

At some point Lynn realized that Jim had switched to using the thick leather strap, but she didn't remember the transition. All of the sensations were fusing together in a continuous sine wave of painful sensuality. She moaned in protest as he removed the vibrator, leaving a hungry emptiness between her legs, and he chuckled as her body and voice begged for it back. Striking her hard again with the strap, Lynn felt the soft material of his slacks like sandpaper against her tender wakened skin as he pressed against her. The warm hard bulge of his cock was pressing between her cheeks, and she pushed back, grinding against it, hoping against hope that he would just fuck her, just use her, but deep inside she knew that thought for what it was. It was her own selfish desire, and she took a greater satisfaction from the way Jim slaked his own lust his own way –

even if that way was enjoying her desperate, panting need to be fucked. He thrust against her, his hips adding a thuddy impact as the strap continued to crack against her fleshy cheeks. Abruptly she felt a slender invasion as he pushed his thumb deep into her ass, and she arched her back with pleasure, her ass driving up against him, trying to show him how much she wanted to be fucked, any way he liked, just fill her...

Then he was gone, and she was left grinding against thin air, hips gyrating towards nothing. Lynn was confused, and peeked over her shoulder, wondering what had happened. Jim stood there, the bulge in his slacks more than evident. "Get over here and take off my belt, slut," he ordered, and she scrambled to obey. She lay the thick leather belt on the bed and folded his slacks without thinking, laying them on the dresser next to the still-slick vibrator. The his hand was at her neck again, pushing hcr down on the bed, ass upright.

"Do you want my belt, girl?" Jim demanded. "Do you want my belt on your ass?"

Lynn was beyond words, but managed to nod meekly, her legs starting to tremble with anticipation. This was new territory, not the familiar toys her master had used on her.

This was an atavistic level of spanking, reaching back to her earliest memories of punishment, of being helpless under authority, and she shivered as she heard the whoosh of the belt as he swung it through the air, landing it in a burning horizontal stripe in the middle of her round cheeks. The noise shocked her more than the pain at first, a loud meaty smack that seemed to echo in the room. Then the slow ooze of pain began to sink deep into the muscles of her ass, and she let out a low, keening sound of surrender. Again the belt came down, and she closed her eyes tight as tears began to fill them.

The her eyes flew wide open as she felt her pussy filled again, this time with a hard, unyielding irregular shape. It took a few moments, even as she delighted in the feeling of it sawing in and out of her cunt, before she realized what it was. Jim was fucking her with the handle of the same hairbrush he'd started with. He must have seen the realization in her face, because he laughed aloud. "That's right, dear Lynn," he said.

"Sometimes the things that bring us pain also bring us pleasure."

He pulled out the brush and laid it on the bed in front of her mouth. Instinctively she sucked it into her mouth, tasting her own sweetness that coated the handle, drawing it deep like a pacifier. She closed her eyes, filling her senses with the taste of her pussy, the hard wood under her tongue, the slight touch of his fingers on the red-hot sizzle of her skin where he touched her ass. Then she felt a thicker, meatier touch. Jim was hard, his bare cock pushing against the side of her ass as he slapped her with it. In spite of the heat it felt almost soothing, the steel silkiness of his erection a solid thud against her cheeks as his fingers filled her, ass and pussy, her mouth filled with the fucking handle.

She sucked and moved under his hand, feeling a primal scream filling her mind, wanting to wrap that cock in a condom and put it where she so badly needed it.

Instead he roughly pushed her over, the coverlet giving an instant of cool ease to her burning ass cheeks and thighs before turning into an abrasive caress. Straddling her chest, she could see his cock, filling her vision as he stroked it, inches from her face. Her mouth and legs both opened in vain, wanting to take the cock in, but Jim just tantalized her with it, one hand caressing himself while his other hand reached back and fingered her cunt even more. Her hips bucked up at the sensation, trying to draw his hand deeper, wanting to fuck him so bad that she couldn't even voice the words.

Jim was watching her face, watching her watch him touch himself, stroke after stroke, and his whisper filled her head. "I'm going to cum on you, slut," he said hoarsely, his hand starting to speed up. "I'm going to cum all over your sweet tits. How will you like that?"

Lynn moaned, still too far gone in lust to speak. She arched her back and lifted her breasts with her own hands, offering them to him, her body a willing altar to his desire.

Jim's hand became an urgent blur and he grimaced, a low hiss forcing between his teeth before it became a growling, triumphant roar. He shot his cum all over her chest, and as Lynn felt the hot jism hit her skin she instinctively began rubbing it into her skin, wanting him to cover her, to engulf her outer self even as his spanking had taken over her mind. This was new; she'd never done anything like it before, but there is no thought behind it beyond the sensation of being overtaken by the sensuous stimuli.

She wanted to cum so bad.

An eternity later, she heard a sound. Eventually she realized it was a voice, and a bit later managed to sort it into words that she could understand. It was Jim. "Get out of bed. Get dressed."

She opened her eyes, looking to her Master now that the scene with Jim was over.

Surely he could see how much she was in need of release? Perhaps he would simply rise from the couch, come to the bed, take her and make her his again and again.

Perhaps – but it was not to be. Her master was simply sitting on the couch, still, waiting patiently as if nothing had happened.

Lynn got out of bed then, quickly, and got dressed, the drying cum making her dress stick to her in odd places. Her thighs slid against each other, still wet with her need. She ran her fingers through her hair in a vain attempt to bring some order to her coiffure, feeling them shaking with unassuaged sexual desire. What made it more intense was the knowledge that her master could see all of these things, and that he knew just how badly she wanted to be fucked – and that she would do whatever she was told, nothing more, nothing less.

She stands, silent, head bowed slightly, as the men shake hands, Jim thanking her master profusely. "Quite a little slut you've got there. You should take her home and fuck her."

She feels her Master's eyes on her, and she can't help but smile a little. "I just may do that," he says, opening the door. "I think she's earned it."

As they walk out of the hotel, he took her hand. Lynn's breath caught a moment before coming, deep and strong, filled with the lust and joy of being his.

GETTING STARTED

Dan says

How will you get started with your slutty life? What will be the point where you are open to the idea of grabbing someone by the hair and demanding your cock is sucked...or where you are open to having your hair grabbed and 'forced' to take it (and smiling at the delight and desire it brings).

A couple of definitions

First off, you need to develop the understanding that you are not a sick fuck, and that kinky sex is not perverted.

It helped me greatly to understand two definitions, kinky sex and perverted sex. And I'll toss in one more, slut, because we use it a lot in this book.

Kinky sex, be it anything from orgasm denial, sexual humiliation, boy and girl and boy tangle ups, or being forced to beg for cock, is just kinky sex. It is just something that 'normal' people don't do (or don't admit to). And the key to everything in our book, every reference to kinky sex, is that it does not harm anyone. It does not harm the people directly involved, as they are consenting adults. It does not harm anyone indirectly involved and therefore, it does not (in our view) include cheating. Simply put, it is any agreed to act with any number of people (or devices) that is done with integrity.

Perverted sex is everything else; or said in another way, sex done without consent. Rape, minors, and animals excludes consent and does cause harm and is therefor, in our definition, perverted. Now, we could get into this and argue here and there (are two 17 years old's exploring each other perverted? Was the goat really harmed, he seemed to enjoy it....) but we are going to keep it simple and stick with our definition. The key points are consent and not doing harm – how freaky can you be without manipulation and harming another person.

Slut is a word that has caused dawn harm in the past, yet we have reclaimed it and use it both for erotic purpose ("you like it like this, don't you slut?") as well as for empowerment. For us, slut is simply a person (man or woman) who accepts their sexuality as a goodness, no matter what form it takes, and measures the value of it from the inside out (as opposed to letting society judge it), and who has the courage and willingness to explore it. Although a pretty long definition, an easy concept: I am a sexual being, I like sex, I like kinky sex, and I am ok with that. Matter of fact, I'd like to get to know it better. Come play with me.

A bit about how Dan got started

I was actually raised pretty normal in a normal American home. I remember the first time I jerked off and that I felt mildly guilty (and scared – that felt too good to be normal!). I remember finding an old porn magazine in a torn down building and keeping it, and I remember going through my dad's collection as well (there was a book about a wife and a football team I remember fondly). Somewhere along the way, I got married and had a pretty normal life with pretty normal sex. I had the standard fantasies for an American male (which was pretty much two girls at once) but never expected anything to actually happen. Time went by, I got divorced and married again, but it was pretty much the same story – nice normal sex, maybe a bit of dirty talk here and there. So nothing in this so far had led me to think that my sexual life would ever amount to anything other than every other guy at work that I talked to. Adventure was getting some on the side or stopping at the dirty book store.

One day, while downloading porn from the internet (again, a nice normal activity), I ended up with some people tied up having sex. And a little bit of looking allowed me to find people have mock forced sex, tied up sex, girl on girl on girl on girl sex, and all kinds of stuff that opened my eyes (and cock) to a world I was not aware of – and that I was stunned turned me on. Spanking, fisting, rope, and more found their way to my computer.

One night, I found myself and a few friends sitting around, comparing porn. And lo and behold, one of the female friends was making ohh and ahh's over some of my more adventuresome porn.

To fast forward a bit, another divorce happened and I ended up married to that 'ohh and ahh' girl, dawn. And we decided right there and then that 'normal sex' wasn't enough. That we were going to be loving, committed, and very naughty.

dawn says

i was going to add my story here on how i got started…but funny, it is very similar to Dan's story. i do remember fantasizing and reading naughty stories of power exchange and kink back in the day of IRC chat rooms and was a little confused as to why that was really turning me on. This was fantasy, real people didn't do this, or did they? I allowed it to turn me on and did some soul searching, chatted with others that were embracing their kinky side and decided that I was going to find a way to explore this. This need to explore kink and power exchange became so strong that I realized that if I did not give my authentic self a chance to breathe and explore and discover the pleasure that could be found out in the big scary world of naughtiness, I would be doing a disservice to myself.

i'm so glad that we found the courage needed to take that step and move through that fear that keeps most people in their fantasies; and it was a huge fear. We were going to move into a world that we had only dreamed of; a world where there weren't many real time role models. Would reality hold up to fantasy?

Luckily it did work out and continues to be the path we travel. We now have our own naughty stories to share, our own memories and our own pictures of our adventures.

How you can get started

Sharing some pictures worked for me. So did sharing stories with the things I was interested in. But we really started moving along when we shared naughtiness in the throes of passion…and then talked about them the next day.

But before you get there, make sure your partner is open to anything at all by having a talk that starts with permission to be honest. "I love our sex, but I have some fantasies I'd like your permission to share with you." Let them know that you are sharing fantasies, not things you want to do. And be ok with them being shared fantasies. That can be very hot in itself. This may lead you to working on planning it out, or your partner might say, "I don't mind us talking about it, but I'd never do it." Or they might say, "I never want to hear about this again."

In any case other than 'never want to hear', the key is to start slow and with lots of communication, and we share a lot about that as this book progresses.

Take your time and keep the thought that this is an adventure in mind.

In the case of 'never want to hear about it', it might be something you can silently masturbate about and let go…or it might lead to a modification of the relationship. How important is your fantasy? Is it a hot bit you want to try…or is it an authentic expression of you who are?

BEACH BAR

April fought the nervous butterflies in her stomach. *It will be worth it,* she told herself again and again, like a mantra. *If it plays out like we plan, it will be SO worth it.*

All her master had told her was that he was going to take her to a bar on the boardwalk – not such an unusual occurrence. But when he'd added "...and you're going to get fucked before we get home," her mind had raced with the possibilities. It had been familiar territory in her fantasies, the kinds of things she'd whispered into his ear during sessions. The thought made her ache with desire, she wanted it so badly, but the fear factor – was she really going to be able to do what he asked? Could she be that much of slut for him? – turned that ache into an tremulous quiver in her belly.

She calmed herself by thinking of him – her master, for several years now, a caring man who was attentive to the needs of her needs – or rather, the needs of his property, both physical and emotional. She would follow his guidelines not only because he desired it, but because her trust in him gave her the courage she needed.

He didn't seem aware of her tiny crisis of doubt as he parked the van near the boardwalk. As she came around the van, taking her proper place behind his right arm, she saw him looking at her intently. For a moment she was breathless as she looked at her master, his silhouette against the starlit sky, the bass roar of the ocean mingling with the treble voices of seagulls wheeling unseen in the night sky. Far in the distance the lights of the rides echoed the soft murmur of people laughing, talking, screaming with joy – but on the boardwalk, it was quiet, only a few people walking along the wooden slats.

April couldn't read his expression, but she didn't try; it was enough that she was there and she was his. She took a deep breath, feeling a tingle of excitement as he touched her elbow slightly, indicating that she should follow him to the bar he'd chosen for the night's adventure.

It is a dark, barely lit by dirty bulbs and cheap colored lights whirling on the ceiling to techno beats. The tone of the room changed as her master led her towards the crowded dance floor, and she realized that several conversations stopped as she walked past the small groups of men talking. She could feel their gazes travel up and down her body, and she shivered a bit, thinking of what they were seeing. She was in a tight mini skirt and skimpy halter top, made of a clingy artificial fabric that clearly outlined her nipple piercing. Aside from those scraps of cloth her tanned skin gleamed in the dim light, looking hot to the touch, and her hair was swept back, revealing her long and graceful neck. She also knew something none of the voyeurs did: her master had forbade her to wear panties.

April felt her pussy swell, wet and throbbing, every time she caught someone looking at her, and she did her best to catch their eyes and smile seductively, occasionally reaching up across her chest with a slight brush against her hard nipples, running her fingers through her hair in a way that she hoped was seductive. She snuck a glance down and saw that the piercing in her left nipple was pushing out the thin fabric of her halter even more, and she shivered, both shy and exhibitionistic at the same time. Looking up again, she caught one of her admirers surreptitiously adjust the crotch of his jeans, and she found herself almost panting, knowing that she was turning him on that much. A slight squeeze on her arm brought her attention back to her master, and she looked up at him fearfully, hoping she'd not transgressed – but no, he was smiling, well aware of her own arousal and that of the men around her. He enjoyed having that which others coveted, and in building the heat in his little slut bit by bit, stoking her hunger for cock bit by bit until she would to anything he asked just to get the release she needed.

As they sat in a booth, both on the same bench but with her closer to the bar, she found herself wondering just how much he had planned of this – was she really just supposed to find three guys at random? Or had he planted men here he trusted to take her? She honestly didn't know, and that uncertainty made her even wetter. April trusted her master not to damage his property – but at the same time, over and over he had shown her that her limits were far beyond anything she'd imagined. She couldn't have possibly come to a bar and picked up a man by herself – but for him, she was ready to find not one, but three men to fuck tonight. She squeezed her thighs together nervously, feeling the deliciousness wetness that was beginning to coat her thighs, making the vinyl seat slick under her bare ass.

"Thank you, Sir," she giggles softly into his ear, "for making sure I didn't have panties tonight."

"Naughty girl..." he smiles back at her. She felt his hand under the table, stroking up her thigh, feeling the smooth shaven skin, his fingers coming away wet.

"Naughty, naughty," he repeats, giving her thigh a soft pinch before bringing his hand back up on the table. Looking into her master's eyes, April searched for some clue, some indication of which men might be safe to approach, but there was nothing but calm patience there. No…there was something more, a smoldering lust as he delighted in her disquiet. As she leaned forward, letting her nipples brush the cool tabletop, she looked back over the dance floor.

"Go fetch us drinks, slut, and make it a good show," his low voice in her ear is like a river of fire down her spine, and she feels her breathing get more shallow.

"Yes, Sir," she replied, then "What would you like, Sir? And what may I have?" He caught the bartender's eye from across the room, and made some quick hand motions. "Jake knows what to give us, slut. You just have to take your pretty ass over there and bring it to me."

"Yes, Sir," she smiled, and slid – literally – off the seat. Letting her hips sway in a raunchy bounce to the heavy beat of the music, she made her way to the bar, again reveling in the lustful stares that followed her. Standing at the bar, she leaned forward, making sure to put just a little thrust with her hips so that the skirt lifted that extra inch to reveal the lower curve of her bare ass. She could hear an appreciative swell of conversation, and she smiled even wider at the bartender, who motioned her to wait a moment for the drinks. She nodded and straightened up just for a moment before she casually lifted a leg over a bar stool. Her skirt rode up her thighs, but she made no move to adjust – she wanted to be sure all her admirers knew that she had nothing but a wet pussy under her skirt. As the drinks were put on the bar in front of her, she smiled and leaned in again to pick them up, giving the grinning bartender a bonus cleavage shot. Then she sat back and spun on the bar stool, reveling in the transgressive flutter of her skirt. She knew that anyone looking had just gotten a glimpse of her shaved and glistening vulva, and it put an extra bounce in her step as she sashayed back to her master.

As she sipped her richly colorful drink, a succulent cherry speared in it, she looked wide-eyed up at him, a naif looking for approval. Before he could say anything, though, her expression changed as she swallowed. He chuckled as her eyes narrowed in surprise. "Sir? I think the bartender forgot to put any alcohol in my drink."

Her master grinned evilly. "That's because I want you fully operational for the night's activities, slut. But Jake made sure that you will *look* like you're on a binge, so be sure to act accordingly."

As she thought about it, she found herself with a grin to match her Master's. "Ooh...that will be *fun*, Master! Can we go dance, sir? Please?" He nodded, then pushed her off the seat unceremoniously. "I'm not in the mood to dance, girl. Find someone else to move that slutty body with."

April resisted the urge to stick her tongue out at him, feeling more brazen than ever as the bass drive thumped through her body. Looking over to their left she saw a trio of men standing, all staring at her, apparently debating who would come over and approach her. She cocked a hip and *moved* her mouth at them, and they shuffled a bit more – not so much nervous as with the potential energy of a herd of bulls about to stampede. Suddenly a little apprehensive, she turned again to her master for guidance. "Sir? I think one of those men might be acceptable...but which should I dance with, Sir?"

He looked up from his drink with a fierce expression, as if angry at having his musings disturbed. "You're such a slut, woman, why not just dance with all three of them if you can't make up your mind?"

His expression was stern, but she saw something else in his eyes – a slight twinkle – and suddenly she realized how perfect a man he was, and how perfect a girl she could be for him. Turning, she waved her fingers at the three men, trying to coax them onto the dance floor, and one immediately moved out to join her. The other two moved to the edge of the dance floor but stop there, seemingly content to watch for the moment.

Deep in the crowd, she turned to begin moving with him, and suddenly he became all hands, using the cover of the crowd to hide his blatant groping of her ass, and April lets herself totally enjoy the attention, thrilled at the unfamiliar grip on the curve of her buttocks. She moved her hips to grind into him as he pulled her close, moaning into his ear with wordless pleasure as his fingers pulled her skirt higher, touching bare skin. They moved and pulsed with their own heat in the rhythmic mass of dancers.

Her master had only instructed her to tease, but April wanted to push further, scraping her nipples brazenly across his chest, goading him into more. She licked his ear lobe, his neck, even went so far as to grab his hips and pull him harder into her, riding his thigh as it stroked deliciously, maddeningly against her wet cunt, barely covered by the skirt. She edged closer and closer to losing control completely when suddenly the song ended, drifting into a beat that didn't have the same primal energy. She smiled at the man, both of them dripping with sweat, and gave him a final saucy pat on his ass as she turned to go back to Master's table.

He gave her a wink as she gulped down her drink, and she realized another brightly-colored cosmo-replica was already sitting there in anticipation of her thirst. She grabbed it and slammed half of it, knowing the other two men would see it and assume she was well on the way to being toasted. As she put the glass down Master winked at her, and she grinned back, basking in the wonder of pleasing he to whom she belonged. Impulsively she leaned into him and kissed him deeply, moaning into his mouth as she felt his finger slide between her cunt lips and deep inside her. He slid it out again, finger dripping with her desire, and slapped her ass casually, sending her back to the dance floor. As she skipped away, she caught a glimpse of him slowly sucking her juices off his fingers, and she grinned even wider.

The second man is waiting for her, and she takes his hand without hesitation and moves onto the dance floor. He took the lead, though, pulling her deeper into the crowd, and she realized soon that he was even less inhibited than the first. He also grabbed her ass, but his hands went right under her skirt to the skin of her cheeks, pulling them apart as he pushed against her and moved into the maddening bump-and-grind. The combination of heat from her core and the night breeze stroking her bare ass made her eyes glaze over, thrilled with the thought of being so totally exposed there on the dance floor.

Then the second man lifted one hand to her halter top, sliding it under the material easily and using two fingers to tug gently on the ring piercing her nipple. April's breath caught, then came out in a low moan as he pinched harder, then harder still. The sensation seemed to come in through the hard nubbin he was torturing and go straight to her pussy with a pulsing need. She needed to be fucked so bad she wasn't sure she could stand up, and she gripped him tighter there in the throng of packed, squirming bodies.

As April looked over the man's shoulder, she caught a glimpse of her Master, sitting alone in the booth. He didn't look lonely, though – rather, she could feel his gaze commanding, controlling her even as she danced with the stranger. She also saw his hand, under the table, and knew that he was touching himself, aroused by the sight of his slut moving there on the dance floor. Her pussy clenched, and she tapped the man on the back, thanking him with a bright, breathless smile before returning to Master.

Leaning in, she pressed her breasts against his strong arm. "I'm so hot, Sir! I really want to fuck these guys...all of them, any of them, I just need..." she trailed off in a trembling whisper as his eyes flashed. She whimpered as he suddenly grabbed her by the hair and pulled her ear next to his lips.

"You want to fuck them? Really? How much, slut? How badly do you want it?" His grip tightened and she found herself unable to speak. "Are you willing to do it wherever and whenever I choose?" His words were slow and measured, but the tone left her feeling as though her bones had liquified.

She managed to nod, slightly, feeling her hair pull deliciously in his grip. She knew she would fuck them right at the table if he told her to, and a part of her hoped that he would.

"Drink this down fast. Then get another one. Now."

April chugged down the drink and almost ran back to the bar, forgetting to put any wag in her stride in her haste to accede to her master's demands. Jake at the bar smiled at her and started concocting another colorful drink, making a show of pretending to stack the alcohol, and April grinned at him merrily, happy he was in on their little game. Turning, she saw the three men still staring at her, and she waved coquettishly at them, her grin turning naughty. She lowered her hands to the hem of her skirt and inched it up, slowly, teasing them with the chance of a flash of pussy. Higher… higher…then her drink was ready, and she let the hem fall with a subtle flip of her fingers that lifted it for just an instant. April wasn't sure if they actually saw her wet slit, but she knew it was all they were thinking about. She grabbed her drink and strutted back to her master with a saucy twisting stride.

"Another drink?" he roared at her, eyes laughing even as his face showed anger. "You slut! You know you can't hold your liquor, what the fuck are you thinking?" His strong baritone carried easily over the sound of the music, and she knew the men could hear. She dared a wink at Master, taking her cue and downing the drink in one long gulp. Gasping as she slammed the glass down on the table, she leaned in and planted a prim kiss on Master's forehead before spinning around and heading back for the dance floor.

She let her walk get a bit wobbly as she grabbed the third man's hand, pulling him deep into the crowded body of dancers. April is so hot she wastes no time, pulling his hands around her and practically mounting him there in the middle of the floor. He grinned wickedly, not believing his luck at getting such a hot slut, and tried to slip a hand up under her skirt. Feeling like prolonging the game just a little longer, April pretended to stumble, foiling his grope, and then flopping her arm clumsily against him to block his grasp at her nipple.

The third man was persistent, though, and perhaps having learned from her master, he suddenly grabbed her by the back of her hair and kissed her, hard. It took April by surprise, and she melted into the kiss, the music fading to the roaring in her ears as her blood pounding through her body. His hand was on her ass, the other squeezing her breast, another sliding across her hip towards her mound – With a shock April's eyes opened, and she realized all three men were now surrounding her on the dance floor, caging her with their bodies, their hands everywhere on her. She moaned and leaned against them, one after another, losing herself to the sensation of their touches, pinches, their hungry mouths and eyes... "Air..." she finally gasped as the music changed again. "I must have air."

"Please...take me back to my friend?" For a moment she was afraid they wouldn't, but then they broke apart, and the third man took her by the elbow to guide her back to her master, his two friends following.

Master rose from the table to greet them. "Drunk again, slut? What a whore. You are such an embarrassment to me. We are going home, now!" He reached for her, and she let herself fall, slipping through his grip into a heap on the floor. Channeling her inner brat, she let out what she hoped sounded like a drunken giggle.

"I don' wanna go, *Suhhrrr.*" She let her mouth slur the last word, almost sounding mocking. "Ah'm haffin...*fuhn!* Wit' mah nooooo friens'!" She waved a hand vaguely at the three men, standing tense and horny over her.

Master's face was crinkled with what looked like anger but April could tell he was fighting not to burst out laughing at her performance. "You are going home with me *now*, slut." He sighed, and looked up apologetically to the three men. "Guys, would you help me get her out to the van?"

The three men glanced at each other, and as one reached down to grab her. She staggered up, making sure her hands were brushing against their asses and cocks, feeling at least two erections before shakily letting them straighten her up.

Her master turned to lead the way, and they hustled her out the door like bodyguards escorting a pop star. As they reached the night air, April began to struggle a little, forcing them to grip her arms and waist tighter. She couldn't help moaning a little more at the delicious helplessness of it all.

As they passed a bench she suddenly went limp again, and the three men staggered, losing their grip and letting her fall across the back of the seat, her ass curved up in the air. The skirt was high up on her ass cheeks, their pale curves lifted behind her. "Oh, *suhrrrr*," she slurred again, letting her voice go bubbly and inviting. "If I've been *baaaaad,* pleeeeze spank me, but don' make me go *home.*" April tried to let her voice sound like a whiny teenager.

"Oh, you are going home, slut, and you are definitely going to get a spanking. You guys up for carrying her to my van?" Again the men nodded quickly at each other, and this time the second guy – the largest – simply slung her up over his shoulders.

As he carried her unceremoniously, she could feel his hands gripping her thighs, slipping upward towards her exposed ass, his fingers darting in towards her pussy, briefly. April heard his low "Fuck, she's wet…" and knew his hands had come away slick as her thighs. She took some satisfaction in that, and in his arousal as his step quickened towards where Master was opening the side door of the van.

"Just toss the drunken slut on the bed," he directed, nodding as April's beast of burden unrolled her onto the mattress on the floor of the van. Master looked at the three men, and cleared his throat. "Thanks for your help, men." Holding a hand out to each, he shook their hands, his smile broadening as he felt her juices on the man who carried her. "I'm Joel, and she belongs to me. I'm glad that you all had fun with her on the dance floor, but as you saw, she really deserves a spanking." He fixed each man in turn with a challenging stare. "Would anyone like to volunteer?" As all three men nodded vigorously, he smiled wickedly. "Well, don't be shy, then. Hop in back. I'll just drive around while you play with my toy. A cock tease like her, wouldn't you think she deserves a good spanking and fucking?" At the chorus of nods and grunts of assent, Master motioned them in with a graceful wave of his hand, closing the door with an ominous slam behind them.

As she heard him get in the front seat, April tried to make sense of what was happening. She looked around at the three men suddenly surrounding her in much more intimidating circumstances than the dance floor, and wondered what was going on. She'd expected to be tossed in the van and spanked and fucked, but by her owner, not by these three strange men…men who were staring at her much like starving wolves look at a sirloin steak.

"Sir…?" she asked, a tremble in her voice.

She was not reassured by the sound of his answering chuckle. "You thought the dance floor was it, my sweet one? After you've spent so much time whispering in my ear how much you want to be fucked by more than one cock?"

April answered with embarrassed reluctance. "Yes…Sir."

"Well now's your chance!" Master said. "After teasing these poor guys all night, it's time for you to pay them back with your special…services." He chuckled again and glanced in the rear view mirror at his four passengers. "By the way, slut, meet John, Steve, and Paul. Guys, this is my cock-loving slut I told you about earlier." He checked over his shoulder before changing lanes and added with a smile, "I told you she was hot."

April was in a state of shock. He *had* planned this, with these three men, all in advance…she smiled happily as she understood just what a sneaky, wonderful man her owner could be.

Master's voice called out clearly to the men in the back of the van. "You can do what you want with her, but I have two rules. One, she must get a spanking." He glanced in the mirror again, and caught April's eye. "And two, she is not allowed to cum." He turned the wheel again, and April could see the tall light poles of a parking lot passing by the windshield. She realized that late at night, in an abandoned parking lot, no one would hear them at all.

John grabbed April's thighs roughly, kneeling beside her and spreading them. "Gotta get some of this pussy," he said and dove down. She gasped as she felt him licking roughly, crying out as he suddenly bit her fleshy wet lips, again and again, almost chewing on her pussy, devouring her. The sensations rode like fire up her spine and she arched, gasping out. His powerful hands spreading her, his ravenous attack on her pussy, it made her feel as though she were being eaten alive. She felt the waves of pleasure course through her, bringing her closer and closer to release.

Suddenly he stopped, climbing up her body and kissing her as deeply as he had eaten her out. She relished the tangy flavor of her own pussy as his tongue explored hers. John broke the kiss and looked at her, eyes burning with lust. "How do you like the taste of your own frustrated cunt, you slut? After the way you teased us on the dance floor…now it's *your* turn."

He flipped her over, pulled up her skirt and suddenly started spanking her ass. There was no warning, no warm up, just his hand spanking her hard. For some reason the punishment suddenly felt incredibly humiliating to April, and she cried out, trying to squirm away, but Steve and Paul held her down, unable to move as John continued to rain down blow after blow. He was berating her as he slapped her ass, "You dirty filthy slut. Treating us like your own personal sex toys. Tease us, will you? We'll see about that." He spanked her even harder.

Steve spoke up. "My turn, John." Releasing her arm, he moved behind her ass, pulling his belt out of his jeans. "Get on all fours, slut. Time for your belting." As she lifted onto her arms, tears fell along her arms, and John moved around to her face, taking his stiff cock out from his zipper.

"You may not get to cum, but that doesn't apply to us!" he laughed cruelly at her watering eyes. She could tell even without the hard cock bobbing before her mouth that spanking her had turned him on incredibly. "Suck my cock, you slut, and don't stop until you taste my cum down your throat." Simultaneously he shoved his erection past her lips as Steve brought the belt down on her ass with a loud snapping sound. April reacted instinctively to the pain on her skin by lunging forward, away from it, which drove John's cock all the way down her mouth and throat. She let out a muffled *Umf* that would have been a scream had her mouth not been full.

Steve continued to take his pleasure beating her ass with the belt as John began fucking her face with long deep strokes. His friend Paul was stroking his own cock slowly, eyes wide, seemingly mesmerized by the welts on her ass turning deeper red with each strike of the belt. Steve's cock was tenting his pants as well as he took a moment to run his hand over the raised crimson curve of flesh under him. He could feel the heat coming from her skin, throbbing with her heartbeat, and heard her cries as his friend John continued to pump his cock between her lips. Suddenly he felt her move under her hand, pressing against it with unmistakable desire. Moving his hand between her cheeks, Steve felt the hot slick wetness there, and realized it was not just her ass that was on fire.

He lifted the belt again and brings it down hard, then again. After two more he dropped it, fumbling at his pants and murmuring "Gotta have some of this sweet ass *now…*" She heard the familiar sound of a condom wrapper being ripped open behind her.

April moaned around John's cock, feeling wanton as he fucked her face harder, driving her head down on his member with a strong hand tangled in her hair. He paused for a moment, and she wondered if he was about to cum, suddenly realizing that she was desperately hungry to taste him, to satisfy his lust and swallow his seed. Then his grip tightened again, and he rammed his cock even deeper down her throat, mashing her nose against his pubic hair and muffling her scream of pain and pleasure as Steve simultaneously drove his cock into her well lubricated cunt. They both plowed into her hard and she felt oddly as if she was floating, suspended between these two iron rods of flesh, unable to do more than open her throat and her pussy to their demands.

Steve pumped her hard for a few strokes, then pulled out and slid the glistening head of his cock over her tiny rosebud of an asshole. Instinctively she clenched, hearing him chuckle as he watched her pucker, and she flinched as she realized what was coming next. She tried to relax and shifted her focus to licking John's balls as his cock slid into her mouth, feeling them tighten. She knew he was about to cum, but her excitement was interrupted by the inexorable invasion of

Steve's cock pressing slowly into her ass. She moaned as the sphincter stretched wide, taking him in, and the vibration of her throat was too much for John, who let out a feral growl as he began to cum.

Steve took this as the cue to forego subtlety and just drive deep into her with all his smooth length, filling her completely. He holds his cock there, watching her gag on John's cock that was filling her throat and mouth with cum. April tried to pull back for air and was simply impaled further on Steve's cock, and he grabbed her hips to hold her there, shafted deep, as his friend John finally released her head and fell back onto the mattress with a satisfied thump.

Paul seemed to snap out of his reverie then, moving forward. "I want that cunt. Gotta have it. Let me in there, Steve." Agreeably Steve pulled out, his condom-slick cock still shiny with her natural lubrication, sticking straight out from his jeans. Paul wasted no time, sliding under April before she could think to move from her position on all fours. Quickly unrolling a condom over his thick cock, he forced her legs further apart, until she straddled him, her pussy sliding down onto his cock as her mouth uttered an incoherent sound of pleasure and need.

Steve shifted back behind her and slid his cock back into her ass, the feeling even more wonderfully tight now that Paul's hard cock was filling her slut-hungry cunt. As he pumped her ass, Steve gripped her hips harder, feeling the cum boiling up from his balls. "Tight, horny little ass-slut," he murmurs, his words blurry with the intensity of sensation.

April was groaning, breathlessly whispering "Yes…more… ram this whore harder, fuck me, fuck me with your cocks, harder… spank your little whore, sir, I've been so *bad* sir, please…" She felt Steve pause a moment, then his grip shifts and suddenly his hand came down hard on her left cheek even as he rammed into her.

"Haven't had enough, slut?" he asked, timing each whack of her ass with a hard thrust of his cock. "You just need more of this, don't you?" Steve's hand came down bruisingly hard on the marks his belt had left, each heavy blow driving her deeper into sub space where she took the pain and pleasure for her master. As he picked up the pace of his fucking, the spanks became more rapid, sharp slaps alternating cheeks with a fast tattoo of his palm on her skin.

She began to call out louder. "Oh thank you, sir! Thank you! Fuck this slut, spank me, bite me…use me, use this slut hard!" Steve rammed her even harder, spurred on by her words, and Paul matched his friend underneath her stroke for stroke. Every spank had sent a tremor through April's pussy and around Paul's cock, driving him wild with the sensation of her entire body vibrating on top of him.

Finally he grabbed her hair and stilled her words with a kiss as his cock exploded into her pussy.

Steve felt his friend's cock pulsing inside of April and it sent him over the edge as well. He stopped spanking her long enough to grab her hips and drive as far into her ass as he could, deep within her, spurting his semen, gripping her so tightly that his fingers left bruises as he came with a shuddering primal yell. Catching his breath then, he gave her one last spank and stumbled back against the wall of the van, pulling up his pants.

Master's voice came matter-of-factly from the front of the van. "Roll off Paul, you cum-filled slut, and let them get their clothes back on. I have to take them back to the bar."

April's body responded to her master's orders instinctively, but as she lay there it took a while for the meaning of what he said to register with her consciousness.

"Back to the…but…Sir…"

"No buts," Master's voice was uncompromising as he turned the ignition and the van rumbled to life. The men quickly peeled off their used condoms and tossed the used latex carelessly on top of her, one draping over her breast while the other splatted wetly against her belly. "Keep your legs wide open. I want them to see how slutty you are with their condoms and cum dripping out of your mouth, your snatch and your dirty little whore's ass still stretched wide."

She lay there, feeling the hot cum ooze out of her stretched holes, the taste of John's seed still in the back of her throat. Watching the men quickly dress, she felt humiliated and aroused as they looked at her and grinned. She knew they saw a hard-used slut, who hadn't even been allowed to cum, and without thinking she touched herself between her legs, fingers coming away with a daub of her own juices still thick and juicy. Her eyes glazed as she touched her breasts, squeezed her nipples, still wanting more, needing more, but her legs remained spread as her master ordered. Opening her eyes, she saw the men were looking at her differently now – measuring her, as if speculating how they could take her again. Then the van pulled into the bar, and with regretful, wistful looks, they got out of the side door as her master opened it.

She heard him thank them profusely for fucking his girl, just before he slammed the door and got back in the van. There was silence in the sex-filled air as he pulled away from the bar.

Finally her master glanced back at her lying there, well-fucked and awaiting his pleasure. "OK, my slut," he said warmly, and she basked in the approval she heard in his voice. "Since you're all hot and wet, I think it's time to show you what else I have planned for you tonight…"

ON BEING A NICE SLUT'S HUSBAND

"Am I being too slutty?"

One of the underlying principles of many of our activities or fantasies is the ability to be vulnerable and "let sluttiness happen". Like in the story **Hard Paddle,** there are things we can fantasize about doing (and can really want to happen) but bringing them to reality requires a partner we can trust to keep us safe; and also in whom we can trust that after everyone has had a nice sweaty time and a nap, they will look at us with the same love and respect they did before. "Boys won't respect you if you sleep with them" was a lesson that was crammed down our throats, so it is only natural for women to have some concern that they may not be seen with the same affection if they let those fantasies loose. As we were getting further away from 'missionary position monogamy', Dawn would often ask, "Am I being too slutty?" Dan's response was to constantly remind her that they were on the ride together, and were equally slutty.

Part of our journey was taking the very word "slut", which the dictionary simply defines as "a promiscuous woman"[1] and redefining it from a negative connotation to a positive one. Janet Harding and Dossie Easton, in their book "The Ethical Slut", define slut as "a person of any gender who has the courage to lead life according to the radical proposition that sex is nice and pleasure is good for you"[2]. We accept that definition as the Right Way of it, although the words we use are "someone who embraces their sensual nature with integrity."

---

[1]   Merriam-Webster Online Dictionary, © 2005-2006

[2]   Easton, Dossie. *The Ethical Slut: a Guide to Infinite Sexual Possibilities*. San Francisco, CA: Greenery, 1997. Print.

GROUSE FLOGGING

Whoever said Sunday was supposed to be a day of rest didn't marry my husband. His idea of a Sunday involved me draped over a spanking bench, my ass still warm both from his hand and others. He believed in hands-on education, after all, and after demonstrating good spanking technique quite thoroughly, many other people at the demo workshop had wanted to try. That meant I was in La-La Land, ready for whoever was next to try their hand at…me. I closed my eyes, waiting dreamily for the first strike to my already cherry-red ass.

Instead, I felt fingertips touch my side. Another hand started rubbing my ass – and whosever hand it was, wasn't shy. There was no hesitation – this hand knew what it was doing. I felt soft breath in my ear, and couldn't stop the smile from coming over my face. I knew just who this was…and suddenly the evening was even better than before.

It was a guy from OK Cupid who I'd messaged the previous week, telling him I was curious about his "grouse flogging" technique: on the receiving end, of course. He hadn't responded to the message, and I'd not given it much thought, even when I'd seen him and his partner come into our demo. I'd figured it was more professional courtesy than anything else – this guy was not a novice to impact play.

Apparently he'd had an ulterior motive.

As I lay there on the bench, he dragged his fingertips over my back, and I shivered and twitched, letting the low moan escape my lips to let him know just where he was reaching me. My skin felt warm, even exposed as it was, and every inch seemed to expand outwards, longing to be touched. As if he read my mind, he dragged the tails of his flogger softly across my body, the leather strands like warm fingers caressing my neck, my sides, my calves and even the soles of my feet. As they trailed off it left my skin hypersensitized, electrified, ready for what I suspected – what I desperately hoped – was coming next.

I lay my head on the bench, let a cleansing breath out, closed my eyes and prepared to be pleasured. I didn't have long to wait.

The first strokes were small, like the soft beats of an angel's wings fluttering against my hot and hungry skin. He moved them over my shoulders, down either side of my spine, deliciously, teasingly, and inexorably moving to my hips. Stroke after stroke, the soft rhythm lulling me into a trance of pleasure. I knew this was his style, not going for pain – he'd said as much in his workshops. But he also knew that pain very definitely was my style, and I could feel him slowly – agonizingly, wonderfully – ramping up the beats stroke by stroke. No mistaking it – he was making love to my body with the leather.

Then he stopped, and laid the floggers across my neck. The weight seemed to hold me there, and I could feel the warm falls draping around me like the world's sexiest scarf. It was a preview from him, a foreshadowing of what was to come. Again he leaned down to my ear, breathing hot into it, letting his breath follow the same path his floggers had taken. The heat from his body flowed out over my skin like a ghost of molten lava, all of my nerves heightened so that the slightest puff sent electric shivers through me.

Oh, he had me. And he knew it. I could feel his complete attention focused on me, and I knew I had him, as well. But this was just the prelude – I felt his hands lift the floggers again, letting them stroke my neck gently one last time before he stepped back. There was a feeling, even with my eyes closed, of the potential energy gathering as he centered himself and prepared for the dance.

A couple of soft strokes hit, but quickly, as he moved up my body, they became more intense. I moaned again, loud, aware on some level that people were still watching but not caring. Where we were didn't matter, all that existed in that moment was the ecstasy I felt, and I let my voice carry it beyond my body. I didn't moan so much as I *was* moaned, as each strike of his flogger drew sound from my lips and pleasure from my core. There would be the sudden connecting slap of the leather against my skin, then the drag as it was drawn back, the soft leather beginning to feel more rough as my skin became raw. *SLAP…drag. SLAP…drag.*

The beats became faster as he moved into a Florentine figure-eight style, gracefully increasing the rate of the blows but still keeping the intensity in that gray area between pleasure and pain – or, in my case, pleasure and OHMYGODYES pleasure. There was no room for pain in my trance, in this dance of flying leather and breathing skin and fiery nerves and rhythmic connection.

I floated higher, buoyed by the sound of my own moans, lost in the mesmerizing pattern of his strokes. At the same time, every impact brought me deeper into my body, from the burning of my skin to the wetness that covered my thighs to puddle on the bench at my knees, making them slip as I writhed under his steady arm. My eyes were rolled back in my head, my breath a hoarse, ragged pulse of incoherent sounds.

Suddenly another sensation was added, as I felt hands on my feet, digging in to the soles with every strike of the flogger. Every stroke of the leather falls was accompanied by a strong dig into the meridians there, sending jolts of sensation from my inside out even as the flogger worked from the outside in. I was almost completely gone at that point, feeling my consciousness fading into something else – not unconsciousness, something made of primal pleasure and raw need. It never even occurred to me to wonder who was doing this to my feet – it simply was *happening.* Higher and higher, the room, the people, the entire fucking planet faded from my awareness as I was engulfed by that sea of sensation. The sound of the leather striking my skin, my breath, my long keening moans…

The peak of the dance was an endless moment of blinding pure no-thought. It lasted forever and not nearly long enough.

He slowly began to take me down. I wanted to protest, *Oh… I'm not done…I want more…please…* But there were no words left in me – it would take me a while to find language again. A master of his craft, he took me down slowly, mixing in hand strokes with the beats of the flogger, his warm skin against mine like a sweet balm, kissing me with touch everywhere the leather kissed me with force. Slowly, slowly, he brought me back along the path to coherence, until his hands had touched everywhere, and he laid the floggers across my back. I could feel my heart sending pulses of heat through my throbbing skin.

Bending close, he brushed the hair from my face and whispered, "The Goddess thanks you for your gifts…" The breath left my body with a beauteous sigh at the relaxing power of those words. Moving to the other side, he repeated the gesture, gently drawing back my hair and breathing into my ear, "Mother Earth hears your voice and thanks you for the healing energy." I could feel the love of the earth, of every creature on it, as he caressed my back, and he concluded with a final soft murmur, "I thank you for the sensual, glorious gifts you have shared with me."

We stayed there, together, for a while, his hands gently stroking, touching, helping me come a little more back to myself with every breath. Finally he helped me off the bench, to a shakily standing position, and I lifted my eyes to him. Words seemed inadequate to what we'd shared, so I simply said "thank you." as we wrapped each other in a heart hug. I felt our energies melt into each other, and a little part of me found the right word: *Wow.*

When time returned, he needed to find his partner, and I spicily waved him off, assuring him that I wouldn't try walking until I was really able to. The pool sounded like a good plan, cool water for my still-burning skin, and I made my way there, still smiling, still feeling connected to him, to the leather, to everything and everyone.

Stripping, I let the waters envelop me. It is exactly the right sensation, exactly the right moment. I didn't care that I never get my face wet, there was no room left in me for fear – only for love, for joy. I listened…the sound underwater is exactly the color of rapture.

Finally I rose from the pool, lazily threw on a towel and saw him with his partner, close by. I let my towel drag over her feet as she lay there on her belly, sunning lazily, and she smiled up at me as I lay my hand on her shoulder. "Thank you," I said to her, wanting to acknowledge her part in allowing he and I to share that experience. With my other hand, I touched his shoulder, completing the connection.

At that moment, I didn't know if I'd ever see either of them again. But it didn't matter.

This was a slice, just a glimpse, of paradise. And that was heaven enough for me.

MIND OF LUST

Part 1 – Mindless Lust

Dan says

We worked long and hard to develop trust. With that trust between us, it allows us to seek adventure. Personally, the idea that my significant other gets to the point of 'mindless lust' or, at other times, 'mindful lust', is very erotic to me.

Mindless lust is when I've teased her so much and gotten her so hot that she is willing to do anything in the midst of passion. During an erotic encounter, I will play with her, use her, do those things that I know excite her the most, and at the point I am ready to fuck her, make her "prove" that she has reached the level of sluttiness that her critical or conscious mind is no longer part of the picture, that her raw desire is all that is left. I will tell her that if she wants me to fuck her, she must first beg me to let another man fuck her. We both enjoy fantasy and erotic talk, so it was easy – and hot for her – to respond with "yes, yes please let other men fuck me."

In later sessions, I'd make her specify a man by name. So before she could have my cock, I'd hear "please let Steve fuck me, I want his big cock in my pussy, I need fucked so bad." Later we would run into Steve, and my wife and I would exchange a glance, and she would blush for what seemed to be no reason.

One of my favorite other variations of this is when she mentions in passing someone that she does not find attractive. On occasion, after leaving a social gathering, we will talk about people we've just met and if she (or I) found so and so attractive or interesting. So, when I want to hear her reach that level of mindless lust, I'll pick the name of someone that she suggested she does not find attractive. So, as my cock is sitting at the lips of her cunt, I'll tell her if she wants me to fuck her, I want to hear her beg for (that guy you found unattractive, lets use Joey this time). As she begins bucking and pleading me to let her fuck Joey, I'll remind her that she said she wasn't interested in him, and she will respond with "I don't care, I need it, I need cock, please let him fuck me, anyone, I need fucked so bad." I'll tell her if I fuck her tonight, she will have to agree to fuck Joey tomorrow, and hearing her agree and beg to be allowed to fuck him drives us both into a frenzy.

The reason mindless lust works for us, is that she understands I gain as much pleasure in making her slutty as she does. That is when I say, "look how wet your cunt is from begging to fuck other men," I am also saying, "you giving me your complete lust is making me hard and want you more and more." Vulnerability is the ultimate aphrodisiac. Further, she understands that, in this case, this is fantasy play, and that the things either of us say are "non-binding". I am most likely not going to call 'that guy' the next day; I will never say to my wife "you agreed to do so and so last night so now you have to go do it." We *may* go do whatever it is we are discussing, but that will be negotiated later. This allows her to let go completely and let her "inner slut" come out and play without fear.

Mindful lust, on the other hand, is a plan to do something normally followed with carrying out that action. We will discuss that a bit later….

(1) All the names mentioned here are probably made up people…but if your name is mentioned and you know us, and it turns you on to think 'Is that me they are talking about?' well…good.

dawn says

Rarrrrrr !!!!

The place we call 'mindless lust' is an amazing place to discover and allow yourself to enjoy! To get to this place involves amazing trust and vulnerability. What can be sexier than that? When he's driven me over the edge of insanity and i know that i'm in a safe place and can let my walls down completely and just be my authentic inner naughty self…what joy! And he does take me to a place where i feel like i'll do anything for him! i can admit to all the dirty stuff that is zipping through my head. i can speak, 'yes! i'd love to fuck him!', mean it, and know that he finds it naughty too!

Do you ever have things that you want to say like that during a hot sex session? Do you hold them back not knowing how they will be taken or not wanting your partner to know just how naughty your thoughts are? With mindless lust, that barrier is broken and all of that lust and passion gets expressed verbally, physically, squishily as you squirm under, or over, your partner!

SHOWER

Julie sighed appreciatively as the hot water poured over her hair, the steam billowing around her. She luxuriated in the feeling of not-quite-scalding streams pounding against her skin, moving her head slowly side to side under the showerhead with her eyes closed.

She heard the shower door slide open, and without opening her eyes she smiled. Every now and then her husband would join her, and she wiggled a little under the water in anticipation as he slid in behind her. She tilted her head back and let his strong hands finish rinsing her hair, letting out a soft "hmmmm…" of delight at the attention. She could feel the teasing brushes of skin against skin, his cock against her thighs, her nipples kissing his chest as he moved her body, washing her. She loved the feeling of the suds as he washed her, his fingers sliding over every part of her. Again her body gave a little wriggle, like a cat being stroked, and as he turned her under the shower, rinsing the last of the soap off her body, she leaned into his chest with a contented sigh, pressing her body full-length against his, loving how they fit together.

He tilted his head forward and whispered into her ear. "I have a surprise for you." Before she could react, the shower door opened again, and another body entered. Julie froze in shock, confused. There was someone else in the house? There was someone else in the shower with them? Before she could move and face the stranger, she felt her husband's hand on her neck, keeping her from turning her head. Instead he tilted her gaze up to look at him – and she saw him smile. Something in that smile drove her fears away, leaving only the anticipation and excitement of whatever was coming next.

The stranger's body pressed against her back, sandwiching her deliciously between him and her husband, and she felt unfamiliar hands grasp her hips, new lips nuzzling at her shoulder. She was certain that it was a "he" as his semi-erect cock brushed against her naked ass, slick with streams of water running down between them both. A shivering tingle went up her spine in spite of the heat, and her body was still tense, but slowly relaxing under the ministrations of the two men, her husband and…who?

The stranger's hands slid back from her hips to cup her ass, moving up to massage her sacrum, while her husband massaged her shoulders, her neck, breathing softly into her ear. As her body relaxed more, Julie realized he'd planned this little surprise, just a bit different than their usual play. She'd been with other men since they'd been married, just as her husband had enjoyed other women. They'd even done some partner swapping with other couples on occasion. But this was different – another man touch her while her husband not only watched, but participated, that was a whole new level. She closed her eyes and could feel her husband's cock getting hard, pressing up between her legs.

This was a *good* level.

He pulled away, gently, whispering "Keep your eyes closed. I'll see you in just a bit." She felt just a tiny *frisson* of excited fear as he slid past her body and out the door, leaving her there with the stranger. The unknown man leaned in from behind her, his voice as sensual as his hands on her body. "Lean against the wall."

She obeyed his gentle command, putting her arms up against the cool tile to cushion her face. She smiled as she pictured how she must look – this posture pushed her ass out provocatively, and she hoped the new guy would appreciate the view. She heard him soaping up his hands and her smile widened as he began to lather her body slowly, methodically. His hands criss-crossed her breasts, playfully pinching the nipples with slippery fingers that made her want to giggle. They slid down her belly and he stepped closer, rubbing his own body against hers, cock against her ass, his length a teasing, hardening pressure along the cleft of her ass. She moved backwards, grinding back against it, as his hands dip lower, soaping up her pussy. As his hands delved between her lips, her own slickness mingling with the soapy bubbles, she could feel him grow harder, press even more firmly against her, and she moaned. She felt divine, leaning there against the shower wall, divinely slutty because she had no idea who this man was but she didn't care. *So slutty,* she thought as he continued to lather her skin.

His hands spread Julie's ass cheeks and he slowly and deliberately pushed his thumb past the tight little hole and into her. She moaned again, arching her back more to push her ass out, against the welcome intrusion. He moved it deliciously inside of her, and she gasped as his other hand tangled in her wet hair and pulled her head back, hard, her spine now curved almost in a C-shape. She bucked back against him, reaching a more primal level of desire. He pushed up against her again, mouth close to her ear. "If you're good, maybe I'll fuck this for you later." She can feel his cock like a hot iron rod pressed against her, throbbing with expectation, but she can't do more than whimper to let him know how much she wanted to be good, wanted to be fucked right then and there.

Pulling out, he quickly rinsed her off and smacked her ass lightly, pulling her back against his broad chest again for a moment to bite at her neck. With quick efficiency he slid open the door and guided her out. Though her eyes opened as she stepped out, she couldn't focus and his hand on the back of her neck kept her from turning around. She has just enough time to see her husband standing there, naked and smiling, before he lifted his hands with a blindfold and took away her sight again.

"I could hear your moans all the way in here, slut," he said as he ties the knot tightly at the back of her head. The other man – the man she's yet to even catch a glimpse of – toweled her off roughly, the texture of the cotton towels wakening her skin even more than the steaming water had, and Julie could feel her heart pounding even more.

She felt their strong arms lead her to the bed, her bare legs pressing against the foot of it. Somehow the hands seemed disembodied as they pulled her down, bent over, her hands on the edge of the mattress. The blindfold was thick, there was no light, and though she knew she was in her own bedroom with her own husband, the environment seemed strange, alien, filled with unknown sensations and potential. Shivering a little, Julie tried to relax into the feeling, trusting her husband to guide her through this adventure.

She felt strong hands rub her ass even as the mattress in front of her dipped with the pressure of someone getting on the bed. Her mouth opened slightly in an *"oh"* of delight as she felt the tip of a hard cock brush her mouth. Eagerly she opened wide, questing, finding, and letting the cock muffle her happy moan as it slid deep into her throat. As if in answer, the hands at her ass gave her fleshy cheeks a light slap, making her moan again. She focused on giving the best head she could, running her tongue up and down the length of the shaft, swirling her tongue across the tip, and found herself rewarded with him pushing harder down her throat. Julie loved the taste of this man, different than her husband, and she tried to relax her throat, letting him drive even deeper. The hands at her ass spank her more, warming her cheeks as the blows came harder and faster.

Julie reveled in the sensation, thinking for a moment how her husband had outdone himself. She'd been asking for a double-penetration experience for a long time, but never thought it would happen. To have it happen like this, no warning, enabled her to truly sink into the fantasy turned reality, no room for self-consciousness as the two men focused on her. She wiggled her ass again under the spanking, loving the slutty feeling that coursed through her. She could feel waves of heat coming from between her thighs, and she wished that someone would take the hint and touch her swollen cunt.

The men seem content with fucking her face and slapping her ass, though, and the taste of the man's precum is sweet and tangy, so *male* but so unlike her husband. She's never seen this man, but she's devouring his cock like a sex-starved trollop, and loving every second of it. The thought of her husband watching her go down on the stranger sent a new thrill through Julie's mind and she redoubled her efforts. Her mouth slurped and licked and sucked at the hard flesh before her, blind to it but knowing every vein and curve with uninhibited intimacy. As she sank deeper into her role as the wanton hussy, Julie's cunt became even more wet, dripping down her thighs. Oh, she hoped someone would fuck her soon.

Suddenly the spanking stopped, and she shook her ass in protest without missing a stroke as she sucked the stranger's cock. Suddenly she hears a rough whisper in her ear, too low to know if it's her husband or the stranger. "You may not be able to see what is going on right now, but you will later, you beautiful slut." Suddenly she heard the unmistakeable click of a camera shutter, and she froze. *A camera?* Suddenly she was caught up in conflicting emotions, residual shyness and self-consciousness warring with the exhibitionist slut demanding *Yes!*

For a moment she wondered if perhaps things had gone too far. Then the stranger whose cock was still in her mouth took the initiative by grabbing her hair and fucking her mouth, his pumping cock using her mouth in a totally different way than her sensual oral artistry a moment before. The feeling of being used so blatantly helped Julie's inner slut drive away any doubts, and she surrendered to the moment, letting the fantasy take over, her clit seeming to twitch and tingle with every snap of the camera.

Julie couldn't do more than try and keep her mouth open in a tight *moue* around the cock as the stranger face-fucked her. She felt a surge of joyous pleasure as her ass was taken in hand again. A small part of her mind was suddenly taken by a new idea. *Two men...four hands occupied... who's taking pictures?* Even as she adjusted to the idea that she really had no idea how many men were in the room, she felt two more hands stroking her back, lightly. *Six hands...and still the camera is clicking.*

Her ass was starting to have that wonderful slow and deep burn that came from a long spanking, each slap coming harder than the one before. The hands on her back reached down and began playing with her breasts, and she could feel the cock in her mouth slow, throbbing. She knew he was close, and she moved her tongue against him, willing him on. The smacks on her ass got harder, driving her forward on his cock with every blow, making it sink deeper in her throat. Suddenly she heard him groan and he pulled out, leaving her swollen lips pouting with need and abandon. The camera clicked furiously as he roared with climax, shooting load after load of semen over her face, her hair, her neck. "Yes, yes, yes!" she whimpered, eyes closed and mouth eagerly open to catch his cum.

After the last sensuous rope of jism landed on her left cheek, the camera stopped, and she heard a voice – a male voice she didn't recognize – moan appreciatively. "I need to *fuck!*" he said, and after a moment of shuffling a new set of hands grabbed her hips. Julie felt his cock slam into her swollen cunt, ready and wet with need.

"Yes!" she screamed out as she felt the man behind her begin thrusting wildly, hard and deep inside of her. Suddenly the bed shifted again, and her voice was muffled again as another cock thrust into her mouth. Julie no longer wondered who it was – her husband, the stranger, the cameraman, she didn't know, didn't care. Behind the black blindfold she was simply a slut, these were simply cocks and that was all that mattered. They were using her, these beautiful hard cocks, fucking her mouth, her cunt, even as the camera again snaps in the background. Her moans gave way to guttural, hungry sounds as the man behind her pounded harder, and the cock slipped out of her mouth for a moment, sliding along her chin. Julie grabbed it hard, pulling it back between her lips, sucking and licking voraciously. The beautiful wet sounds of her cunt and mouth merged as she lost control, no longer knowing where her body ended and another began. Her cunt and her mouth and the cocks and the camera and the sound of hands on bodies, hers and their own, it all became a mélange that took over Julie's mind completely.

She felt both disembodied and wonderfully, totally present in her flesh, used in the most heavenly way she'd ever imagined. As the mindless lust consumed her, both men pulled out of her and she felt their warm cum splash on her ass, her back, her face, still coated by the stranger's orgasm. *Slutty, so slutty...* runs through her mind *They are cumming on me...* while the camera whirls on.

After the men spent their cum, she felt their hands spin her around and lay her back on the bed. For a moment the room was still, filled with the memory of the recent sounds of pleasure. Then the camera shutter snapped again, and Julie felt her own hands, almost of their own accord, moving over her body, down to her pussy. She began to play with herself, twining her fingers around her hood and labia, softly stroking the swollen clit, dipping her fingers into the pool of desire she found there.

She felt someone come close to her ear, and this time she recognized her husband's voice, telling her what he wanted her to say. She spread her legs wider, arching her back up as she stroked her pussy, and begged. "Please…I need more cock. I'll do anything, just give me more. Fuck my cunt, my mouth…Use me. Whoever you are…won't one of you strangers please *fuck me?*"

As she felt the bed shifting, her offer accepted, Julie smiled deep and happy, and gave herself up again to pleasure.

MIND OF LUST

Part 2 – Mindful Lust

Dan says

Our journey into 'mindful lust' began in the bedroom, as many journeys of lust do, with whispered fantasies as we fucked. "I'd love to see you eat another woman" or "I'd make you suck off a stranger" fantasies that we would share to increase our passion. But it could be said that Mindful Lust actually takes place the next morning. When you are spent, and relaxed, and generally happy with life after a great night of sex, and you ask your lover "That stuff you said last night...do you think you would really like that?" This requires a level of fearlessness. You must trust your lover to the point that you can answer. If you are in a normal sort of relationship, you can imagine the peril you might feel at such a question – either being asked it, or at what the answer might be. I can clearly recall the point, sitting calmly and not filled with lust, but just curiosity, when I asked my wife "If I really did find someone, a complete stranger, and made you fuck him or her – tied you up and just made you take it – do you think that would be something that was exciting for you?"

The question asked during sex is easier to answer. We are more vulnerable, our walls are lower, we are more in tune with our sexuality and our "inner slut" so to speak. We have less interest in what society tells us 'nice girls and boys' do and more of a connection to that desire within us.

But asked during breakfast, or the ride to work, or at the laundry…the question becomes more challenging. It becomes a test to relax your inhibitions and see a fantasy scenario in a more realistic light

At what point can you ask that question? At what point is your relationship so secure, or your trust so deep, or your faith in each other so strong, that you can not only reveal your deepest fantasies to your lover, but also to yourself? You must first decide that it will be worth it. Decide that you are willing to be that trustworthy, strive to achieve that level of acceptance in each other. Have faith in your love.

When I am very old and very gray, and my cock is tired and no longer interested in the ladies (or men or whatever my cock goes for at that point), I do not want to sit on a porch and reflect on the things I did not do. I want to reflect on the things I did do, the chances I took, the love I gave and the love I received.

dawn says

When we are in our rocking chairs, holding hands, we will be able to look at each other and say 'remember when'…assuming Alzheimer hasn't set in. If that's the case, we'll probably just sit there with smiles on our faces.

SUSIE'S REWARD

Susie curtsied demurely as her Master's guest took one of the cucumber sandwiches from the tray, eyes lowered and taking note of how many were left. As she turned away to continue her service at the formal tea, she automatically pushed out her ass slightly, letting the tiny skirt lift a bit and show the lower curve of her bare ass. It wasn't a conscious flirtation; she'd been her Master's willing slave for over a year, combining the skills of a house manager with the natural sensuality of a courtesan. Her mind was calculating how soon she'd have to replenish the tray even as she bent at the waist, legs straight, offering both the finger food and a generous slice of cleavage to the man on the settee. "Lovely," the man commented, and she blushed slightly, a small smile crossing her lips. Susie felt a flush of warmth deep inside of her, knowing that her Master would be pleased that his guests had been well cared for.

"Susie." Her Master's voice came from across the room, and with graceful efficiency she shook herself out of her self-congratulatory state, feeling a little shame at the break in her attention. His face, when she dared look at it, showed nothing but pride, and she felt her heart swell to match the throb in her pussy. "You've done well tonight. I'm going to reward you – and my guests – with a play session. What do you say to that?"

Susie almost bounced with excitement and pride. "Thank you, sir! EEP!" The latter noise came when a pair of strong hands grabbed her arms and spun her around, leading her towards the basement dungeon. She'd been their earlier in the evening, when another couple of guests had done an "exhibition" scene, which had left Susie dripping with arousal. She couldn't even have said what it was, exactly, the couple had done; it was simply the connection between Master and slave that made her quiver with excitement.

To be rewarded by her Master for a job well done was the icing on this particular slice of kinky cake, and at the gruff command to "Strip!" when she reached the bottom of the stairs her maid's uniform – what their was of it – disappeared in seconds. As she kicked it aside, buck naked, she reflected for a moment on how her Master had changed her perception of her body.

She'd thought he – and every other man – would only want her if she were the size of a magazine model. She used to agonize over the fact that she didn't look like a TV star, until he nipped the idea in the bud. He forbade her from dieting. "I want my property healthy, so you'll eat healthy," he'd told her. "If I want someone who looks like a lingerie ad, I'll airbrush you and buy some fake tits." It had taken time, but eventually Susie had learned that she could be – that she *was* – a very sexy, voluptuous woman. Diet commercials be damned, her Master had helped her realize in her heart just how sexy she could be, especially at moments like this one, when she could strip enthusiastically for a group of her Master's guests.

To say she was "forced" would have been pushing it, but she was a good slave, and tried to give at least the appearance of coquesttish reluctance as she stood there, naked, the scraps of her clothing scattered at her feet. "On the table!" came the direction, and

Susie obediently climbed onto the large piece of bondage furniture that was in the center of the room. The guests got busy, all of them experienced in the craft of binding, and soon her hands were tightly tied to the rings on the side of the table, her ankles secured to the two bottom corners, her thighs spread wide. Susie kept her eyes closed, and it made the murmur of their voices seem all the louder as she lay their exposed for all to see. The helpless feeling was somehow both a comfort and an arousal, and her cunt responded, before ever being touched. She could feel the juices as they dripped down her lips, deliciously tickling her ass cheeks before they puddled onto the padded leather surface under her. The exhibitionist thrill sent an electrified shiver of excitement from her brain down her spine and into her swelling cunt lips and clit. She arched her back a bit, craving whatever was going to happen next without a clue as to what it was.

Susie's mouth opened slightly in an "Oh!" of surprise when the first touch came, light, shy fingers touching her thighs. *That's definitely NOT Master,* she thought, and realized it must be his other submissive girl. Susie hadn't had a chance to play with her yet, though the new girl had, according to Master, expressed an eager interest in doing so. That eagerness manifested clearly as the girl's fingers twirled in Susie's juices, becoming slick and deliciously warm as they teased and stroked around her vulva. The submissive ran her fingers over the lips of Susie's cunt and gave them a tweak before traveling higher to flick at the swollen clit, peeking out from under its hood like a shy playmate. Susie jumped at the quick touch and let out a moan. Someone in the room giggled, and it reminded her that she was being watched, people could see her vulnerability and slutty arousal, and that just made her even hotter, the juices flowing faster. Susie let her mind drift, not outward, but inward, sinking into the sensations of her body, her pussy, the submissive's beautiful hand as it stroked, petted, pinched.

Suddenly the hand left its ministrations and Susie instinctively twisted and strained against the ropes, trying to find those beautiful fingers again. Her moans again filled the room, but changed to a shouted "*Yes!*" at a sharp painful sensation on her nipple. The pain transformed instantly into waves of pleasure traveling down through her heavy breasts directly to her cunt, and she screamed "*YESSS!!*" again as two fingers thrust inside her, fucking the greedy pussy with inexorable rhythm. Susie felt her entire body flush warm with the multiple stimulations, and she moved her hips wantonly, her hungry cunt wanting to suck the fingers deeper into her. Both her nipples felt on fire from the sharp spikes now, tiny wheels with needle teeth tormenting the delicate pink flesh. When they lift from her skin she almost protested, but then felt them again, this time at the top of her slit, and she realized that whoever had the torture device was going to apply it to her most sensitive areas. "Yes...yes...yes..." she begged, and the murmured gasps around the room – mostly feminine – gave her a savage sense of pride. She knew the women were astonished that she would want this much pain in that kind of place on her body, but she *did* want it, craved it, needed it, knowing that it fed her soul even as her suffering pleasure fed her Master's.

Three fingers slid into her, deeper, even as the spiked wheel traced a path of fire down one pussy lip. Susie became incoherent, her entire world shrinking down to those fingers, deeper, and that sharp, prickly joy that she wanted harder, more...she twisted and strained, trying to experience more of both.

Whoever was using the wheel took it away, but before Susie could protest she felt the warmth of a mouth over her nipple. She couldn't even speak, but the *Oh, yes* filled her mind as the sub nibbled, sharp teeth scraping and pinching the pointed nubs as her three fingers fucked harder. The lips were soft, and Susie could feel the tiny bites almost tentative even as the fingers thrust into her harder. She knew it was the submissive, ministering to her at her

Master's will, and the thought drove her wild, her body arching up, pushing her breast up against the soft skin of the woman's face.

The beautiful sharp wetness of the woman's mouth disappeared suddenly, and Susie felt dismayed. She wanted it back – the tongue, the teeth. Then she felt four fingers cram into her cunt and forgot about nipples, mouths, almost even her Master, her thoughts focused completely on the thick, full pleasure of her pussy. *Oh yes!* Her voice filled the room for the rapt audience. "Yes…yes…yes… more….more! Fuck my pussy! Fuck my slut cunt! Fuck me, *fuck me,* ram your whole hand into me, *pleeeeeaaase*!"

Breathing heavily in between words, Susie tried to convince the woman at her cunt to give her more, to push her whole hand inside of the sopping wet heat at her core. The woman seemed about to comply, and Susie felt the delicious sensation of the thumb sliding along her lips, pushing in, stretching her.

Then the submissive hesitated, her fingers inside Susie's cunt, seeming afraid she might hurt the bound and pleasure-hungry woman. "PUSH!" Susie demanded with furious lust, "*Push your hand into my cunt! Fuck me, fuck me like a slut!*" With that inspiration, the submissive bore down and forced her whole hand into Susie's slick hole.

Susie's eyes rolled back in ecstasy. This was what she craved, the feeling of fullness, of sluttiness, of being wide open for all to see. This feeling of being *used*. She felt the hand start to move slowly, back and forth, twisting side to side. She could feel the sub's fingers opening and wiggling deep inside her. She heard the heavy breathing and gasps of the people around her as they took in the scene.

Suddenly someone grabs her hair, hard, and her breath caught. It was Master. "Do you know how many people are watching you being fisted by another woman? Do you know how many people are watching my slut beg for more? Tell me what you want, slut. Do you want her to stop?" As the word left his lips Susie felt the hand withdraw with a wet slurping noise.

Her plaintive "NO!" was long and mewling, desperation and desire mingling to make her beg. "Please...*please,*" she moaned. Her body writhed, thrusting her pussy up, down, trying to find that hand to fill it again. Her legs were no longer being pulled by the ropes, they were spread of her own volition, wide open, her cunt like a hungry mouth wanting sustenance.

"What does my slut want?" her Master's voice whispered in her ear.

"F-Fuck," she gasped, almost in tears. "To be fucked. To be *fisted*. To be fisted *hard.*" Her voice was almost incoherent.

Master wasn't satisfied with that. "Louder," he commanded, simply.

Susie screamed, then. "FUCK ME! RAM YOUR HAND INSIDE OF ME AND FUCK THIS SLUT!" With that, the hand rammed back into her pussy, and she let out a barbaric "*Yesss!!*" in triumph.

The submissive pounded into Susie's cunt. If not for the bindings tying her to the table, she would have been pushed off, the woman drove so hard. Susie could feel the fist inside hitting the deepest part of her cunt, filling her more than ever. She squeezed, trying to keep the woman's hand inside, trying to keep that fulness forever. The she felt the woman's mouth again, this time on her clit. It was like heaven, a tongue lapping at her fat, juicy clit, stretched tight from that fist shoved deep in her snatch.

She begged her Master again, for a different boon. "Please, Master, can your slut come for you, Sir?" She repeated the words over and over, until they lost semantic meaning and were simply a mantra of her lust, desire, and devoted service. She held on, desperately teetering on the edge of orgasm, wanting more than almost anything – anything but her need to be 'his'.

She heard his voice, low, firm, in her ear, and it cut through the sea of sensation and tormenting pleasure. "Yes. Cum for me, slut. Cum for your Master."

Susie's body was wracked with convulsive shudders as the deep, deep orgasm formed around the hand still thrust deep inside her. It moved with the muscle spasms of her cunt as they pulsed and flowed in tsunami waves through her body and soul. Finally Susie regained a measure of coherence, the hand gone, her pussy feeling warm and throbbing, her mind feeling the same, blank and peaceful.

She had no idea how much time passed, but at some point her bindings were loosed, and while she felt a moment of loss at their absence, the warm blanket that wrapped around her restored the blissful state of post-orgasmic joy. She looked at the person hugging her through the blanket, and saw her Master's other submissive, grinning happily. Susie grinned back, and the two sat there, waiting for enough strength to return to her legs for her to go upstairs again of their own volition. They sat there, smiling, until Susie's Master would decide to use her again.

D/S AS A SEX TOOL

Dan says

In this book, we explore themes of D/s – dominance and submission – to signify the roles we are playing in the sexuality realm. Sometimes we refer to full time power exchange, and sometimes we use the term Master/slave, but overall, we are using the terms to describe who is running the sexual scene, and who is 'receiving' or 'bottoming' for the scene.

The terms are actually inexact to the way we use them in day to day life, but let's leave that alone for a moment.

In a powerful sexual scene, it can often be a great tool to be gifted with the "in charge" role. Instead of worrying about if this is ok or if that is too much or do you really like caramel dripped on your toes, you just "do". The way you get there is sitting with your partner before-hand and negotiating who is in charge, what the limits are, and then the powerful act of granting trust. "No floggers, no public sex, but I am open to anything to do with Bob or things like dildos. Take me where I long to go." For me, I can let go of the worry and just listen to instinct. And after all is said and done and you've had a nice nap, you can again talk about how it went, what could have been better, and plan next time.

There is also great power in the other side – being *not* in charge, and letting go, and letting what happens, happen. If you have a secret desire of being used by multiple people at the swing club or having someone rub your cock but never letting you orgasm, and you have inhibitions, it can be very powerful to say "Whatever pleases you Mistress" and letting someone take you where you need to go.

We recommend safe words (I want to be allowed to scream 'no don't fuck my ass' and have you continue, but if I say 'red' it means really stop, I have a cramp) and the ritual of permission before each journey, as well as sitting as peers after it is all over and reviewing where it went.

The key to using D/s is developing trust and knowledge of your partner. Your partner needs to trust you enough to really let go – trust that you won't push beyond your limits as well as trust that you won't say 'eww ick' after things calm down. And they need the knowledge of what you secretly can and want to endure.

It is a tricky thing, but it has allowed us to explore and being adventurous because it gives a clear path to action and to reviewing things that went great, and that didn't.

Words

dawn and I are in a full time power exchange relationship. We are Master and slave (and authors of a book that reflects that as a lifestyle, Living M/s © 2010). For us, the normal use of the terminology is that Master and slave is our life roles, Dom and sub are our sex roles. Other people use the terms differently and in this book we mix and match. But that is ok, we are the actions, not the words.

WENCH

She arrived at the dinner wearing the most beautiful dress she owned, even though she knew she was only there to serve. She'd been nervous for days, only finding occasional solace in the sure knowledge that she would do her best to please her master.

He had told her that her name for the evening would be simply "Wench," and that her job would be to serve.

To serve everyone.

To serve everyone anything they needed.

"If anyone asks for anything," he'd said, emphasizing the last word, "you are to obey." As the implications of that order had sunk in, her anxious anticipation had mingled with her arousal in equal parts.

As the dinner began, she had been ordered simply to stand silently near the table in case any of the four masters dining there needed anything. *Anything*, she thought, trying not to let her mind go off in the many directions that word could lead. She tried calming her breath, stilling her hands, trying to relax, breathe and be beautiful and serene and ready to serve – no, she reminded herself, ready to *obey*. She tried focusing on the conversation briefly, but that was even worse; her

quick mind had so many things she wanted to contribute, but that was not her role.

Obey.

She found a thin, fragile peace within that thought until it was shattered by the ringing of the small bronze bell in the center of the table. For just a moment she forgot what she was supposed to do, but her feet were already moving, taking her towards the master who was ringing it with a mildly disapproving look on his face. Her heart pounded as she tried to hurry gracefully over to the man who she had never seen before this night. His gray hair belied the youthful mischievousness in his smile, and his eyes seemed to pierce her as he looked over her dress. He wore a white dress shirt with a black tie and a plain leather vest, the simplicity of the style adding to the strength of his presence. It took a moment for her to remember that she needed to speak; even then, the most she was able to come out with was a breathless "Yes, sir?"

"Where's my coffee?" he demanded, eyes flashing with stern impatience.

She felt a surge of relief; this kind of *anything* she could handle. "I don't know, Sir. Would you like me to go check on it?"

"Immediately." He rejoined the conversation before she had the chance to bow, but she did it anyway, turning and doing her best to gracefully scurry towards the kitchen. For a panicky moment she realized that she was leaving all of the masters unattended, but she could see no way around it, and she pushed through the door to the kitchen.

Three other slaves were working there, preparing the meal course by course and getting ready for her to serve it. They saw her face and whispered words of encouragement – the concern and sympathy in their faces tinged by unmistakable relief. "I'm glad

I'm just preparing and serving one course," murmurs one as she precisely dropped two sugars into the cup, exactly as the master liked it. She was a redhead with the tiny breasts and nipples that were standing out hard from her chest. Eyes shining, the auburn slave paused. "Imagine…having to do anything anyone asked…"

The wench felt her own nipples crinkle in response, and she turned with a breathless "Yes…just imagine…" the tray and hurried back to the masters. She looked fearfully around the table, worried someone else might have wanted something while she was gone – but no, all of the men looked satisfied, enjoying each others company, except the one whose coffee she held. He was looking at her, not quite glaring, but obviously waiting for her.

She hurried to his side and set the coffee cup delicately next to him. "Good girl," he said, and she felt a surge of joy at the precious words. "Now, pull down the top of your dress. Show me your nipples."

The wench gulped, the thrill of praise changing into a deeper, more primal thrill.

Her hands, thankfully, knew what to do, and she lowered the front of her dress, exposing the curve of her breasts and the hard pearls her nipples had become.

The master dipped his finger into his coffee and let a bit of the hot liquid drip onto each nipple before leaning down and sucking on it, hard. The wench's breath caught, and she felt dizzy at the direct line of fire from her areola to her cunt, which started to throb with a need she knew wouldn't go away.

Sitting back up, the master smiled at her expression. He obviously knew what effect he'd had. "That's for being a good girl." Reaching out suddenly with one hand, he gave each nipple a hard twisting pinch, his smile hardening as she squealed in pain. "And that's for taking so long. Back to your corner, wench." The master turned back to the table, but paused as he caught sight of her pulling her dress back up. Again his hand flashed out, painfully slapping her hand away.

With no words spoken, she understood the command: *You will remain half undressed, for my amusement.* Bowing her head, she went back to her corner, the lovely roundness of her breasts unveiled for all to see.

It seemed an eternity before the first course came out – somehow standing there half naked made her feel even more the slut than when she served her master fully nude. As the other slaves came through the door and saw her she could see how their expressions changed – wondering what had happened to her, and wondering what might happen to them. She half hoped the masters would put some of the other girls through their paces, but the dish was served with impeccable grace and the all three scurried back to the kitchen with obvious relief.

The wench didn't look at them – she remembered the instructions she'd been given, and picked up a pitcher of tea from the sideboard to make sure the masters' glasses were filled. As she approached the first man at the table, she stood a little straighter – this was a man she had met before at other events.

Master Jack was his name, and the wench had always found him somehow annoying, for no reason she could quite put her finger on. It made her want to serve the tall, thin man all the better, to reflect well on her master. Jack's long black hair gleamed where it rested on his black leather vest, and like the other masters he was wearing a white shirt under it, though he'd left the collar open.

Though she stood next to him with her eyes cast down, she could feel his gaze burning on her, on her tits, and she tried to keep her voice steady as she asked him if he needed a refill.

Jack reached up suddenly and grabbed her by the hair, twisting her head to point at his glass. "Does it *look* like I need a refill?" he growled. His glass was only a quarter filled.

"Yes, sir," she squeaked, her breasts heaving with quickened breaths.

"Then don't ask, just fill it. And don't spill one drop." As she began to pour, though, he lifted the back of her dress and she felt his rough hands clumsily pawing at her ass, pulling her cheeks apart and driving his fingers between her legs. The sudden exposure and violation made her hands shake a bit, and a dollop of tea spilled over the side of the glass.

Jack's growl was a mingle of disgust and triumph as he stood up, one hand smacking hard into her ass even as the other was taking the pitcher away. He set it down on the table and grabbed her by the hair again, and for a moment she was afraid he might slam her face down onto the table – but his iron control held her face millimeters from the spilled tea, instead. "Lick it up, girl," he demanded, and her tongue flicked out, pink and kitten like, trying to clean the tiny puddle.

Her whole body trembled under the force of his grip – no, it was more than that, it was the way his whole demeanor simply overcame her will. She felt his free hand groping her exposed breast, mauling it, squeezing it, and in spite of her humiliation – or perhaps because of it – she felt her cunt lips thickening even more, the throb in her clit deepening.

At last, the puddle was clean, and Master Jack lifted her upright again, releasing her hair and pinching her nipple matter-of-factly before taking his seat and turning back to his meal. Shaking a bit, she curtsied, trying to center her thoughts before moving on down the table.

Her mind was racing. Should she ask if this man wanted a refill? Should she simply refill it? What if he didn't like tea? Her wide eyes were almost imploring as she looked at the next master – another man she'd never seen before. He simply looked back at her calmly, giving no indication of what he expected her to do.

Swallowing nervously, she decided to take a chance. "Would – would you like a refill, sir?"

"Yes, I'd love a refill, thank you for asking," he said, smiling, and she almost fell over with relief. She poured quickly and efficiently, her breath slowing as she began to feel more calm next to the nice man. She darted her eyes to the side, trying to get a better look at him. He was a younger man, handsome, with beard and dark chestnut hair. His eyes – startled, she realized his eyes were looking straight into hers, and she flushed as she was caught out. Still, he was smiling warmly, and his voice was soft as he said "You *are* a fucking slut, aren't you?"

The warm tone made it take a second longer than normal for her brain to process the words – and even as their meaning stunned her, he was up, taking the pitcher out of her hands and kicking her feet apart with his black leather engineer boots.

Her legs spread automatically, and she felt his hands tangled in her hair, drawing her head back to a deep kiss. He put her hand at the crotch of his tight black jeans and she could feel the hot length of his cock hard against her palm. She moaned into his mouth, the throb in her pussy turning to fire, uncontrollable and ravenous, fueled by his hand fondling the soft round flesh of her breasts.

He broke the kiss, but kept his grip on her hair and her tits. "You didn't answer my question..." his voice murmured, still soft but with unmistakable, menacing power.

The wench moaned again. "Yes sir! A slut...*your* fucking slut." Then she stood there, gasping, as with a smile he released her, giving her a slight push away from the table and handing her the pitcher again. As he turned back to his food, she realized that she had been dismissed again and tottered towards the third master on shaking legs. She could feel her cunt dripping at this point, her thighs coated with her juices – no, she thought to herself, the *fucking slut's* juices.

Halfway to the third master she realized she'd forgotten to curtsy to the second, but there seemed no way to gracefully retrace her steps. Hoping the young man wouldn't notice – except for that small part of her that hoped he would, that he would take her roughly again – she approached another stranger, a man who smelled of clean leather and who her master wanted her to please.

"W-w-would-" she stopped, taking a deep breath. "Would you like a refill, sir?"

"No. I'd like something else," he said pleasantly. Eyes twinkling, he asked her "Would you like to get it for me?"

"Yes sir!" The response was immediate and heartfelt. "I'd like that very much!"

She felt herself flush with her need to be of service to these men, with the chance to please him.

"I'd like my cock sucked. Get on your knees."

The wench hesitated, not certain she'd heard right. *Is this really happening?*

He took the tea pitcher from her. "Did you hear me, girl?" The warmth was gone from his voice as he pushed her to her knees, unbuckling the soft leather pants he wore. His length burst from the zipper and she realized, even as he grasped the back of her head, that yes, this was really happening. And this was unbelievably *hot*.

Her lips parted automatically in luscious surprise as he pressed his cock into her mouth. She licked and sucked passionately, hungrily, lips in a sealed O as he fucked her mouth, one hand wrapped with her hair. His grip tightened as he fucked harder, faster, and for a moment she thought he would certainly explode into her throat – but then, with a grunt, he pulled out and zipped up. Turning back to the table, he resumed eating as if nothing had happened.

Shaken to her core, on fire with the need to cum, she stood – or tried to. Her legs seemed not to want to work very well. The final master stood up and came over to offer a hand, helping her up. She was too stunned, still, to do more than look up at him, wide eyed, trying to remember the words she was supposed to say. Something about tea…a pitcher was around here, somewhere…

The master regarded her evenly, a speculative expression coming over his face. "I'm curious," he said in a deep baritone. "How wet are you from all this?" Without waiting for an answer – as if she could have found the will to respond – he started unbuttoning her dress. In spite of everything the others had done, she felt her heart speed up as he undressed her, her eyes wide on his face as he looked over her naked body revealed. Everyone else was watching, too, eating and watching her, she knew, and her legs began trembling again.

He led her over to the wooden table and grasped her hips, indicating with a slight pressure that he wanted her to sit on it. She perched on the edge like it was a dock on a lake, her feet dangling inches above the floor.

"Spread your legs," he demanded.

Somehow, she found her voice. "S-sir?"

"Spread. Your. Legs." He did not sound pleased at having to repeat himself.

Slowly her thighs parted, as if controlled by his words, not her will, and she flushed with renewed shame as she realized everyone was still eating and everyone was still watching as he exposed her even more.

He reached down and drew his fingers in an upward stroke across her labia, his fingers coming away thickly coated with her juices. She gasped, shocked at the intensity of sensation as his hand had touched her. It had felt…delicious, and her thighs quivered with the electric pleasure of just that one caress. The men watching her mattered less and less – she wanted more, craved more touch.

The master held up his hand, showing the evidence of her desire to the others. "Oh, we have a live one here, men. Soaking wet!" Dropping his hand, he slid two fingers easily into her and she moaned, head falling back, eyes closed, her hips bucking up against his hand.

The master sat down, leaning his head in and began licking, sucking, gorging himself on her succulent pussy. She squealed with joyous pleasure, the waves of lust pouring through her as he devoured her whole. She didn't even hear the other slaves come in with the second course, but she caught sight of the auburn-haired slave, mouth open in a gasp of – shock? Envy? Lust?

The wench's eyes closed as she was taken over completely by the master's ministrations, and her cries mingled with the sound of the other masters rising from their seats, moving towards the serving girls with deliberate and lascivious intent as the evening continued.

SENSUAL HUMILIATION

dawn says

Sensual Humiliation can be hard to explain to some. This is because when most hear the word 'humiliation', they think of spitting, punching, slapping and degrading talk. They think about what we call 'ordeal humiliation'. That is not what we are talking about here.

For us, sensual humiliation is a way of drawing out the slutty side of ourselves. Sensual humiliation is about making ourselves hard or wet, about being naughty. Whereas ordeal humiliation is about tearing someone down, though consensually, so that they can build themselves back up. This isn't what we are talking about here. It's not good nor bad, just different. It doesn't personally turn me on... today. Dan does not degradingly call me a 'fat pig' as a form of humiliation. Instead, he'd whisper in my ear what naughty slut I am and then feel me get wet at the idea. It's about building up my slut self – so that she wants to come out and play.

Sensual humiliation isn't something we'd recommend jumping right into. You'll need to know your partner. Dan and i have been together for years and have shared our complete selves with each other. Because of this, he knows what ideas turn me on. He knows what will push me into that realm of erotic humiliation and have me blushing. But, because i want to please him, i will follow through with his commands knowing he won't do anything to harm me. Sometimes it's not the humiliating action in the moment that is slutty feeling. Sometimes it's just humiliating. But, talking about it later and sharing the experience while being fucked; that can be the slutty part.

i like to mention that everyone has words that can bring up bad thoughts or memories. These are landmines that should be avoided. One person may drool over the word 'slut', but may rip you a new asshole if you call them a 'bitch'. You want this type of play to be fun! That is why you wouldn't jump into this type of scene with a stranger. They don't know your landmines. They don't know your fantasy landscape. They haven't whispered in your ear one night how they'd like to see you with someone else and felt your natural response to such an idea.

We have also found that what may be humiliating for one person, may be second nature for another. This could be for a number of reasons, but the 'why' isn't really important in this situation.

'What to do with it' is what is important. Shopping for cucumbers and lube may be mortifying but wetness producing to one person, and not an issue at all to another. Forcing someone to yell out a strangers name or oink like a pig while they are being fucked, could be a complete turn on to one person and totally turn another off. You need to know the characters in a play before you can use them as puppets in their own erotic story.

Another aspect of sensual humiliation that we find interesting is how it becomes a never-ending cycle. Dan does something that feeds my sensual humiliation buttons, which makes me wet, which i become humiliated over, which makes me wetter, which makes me more humiliated, which makes me wetter; well, you get the idea.

Since sensual humiliation is considered a psychological or emotional type of play, and a play that doesn't necessarily take place in a single 'scene', the aftercare for it can be a little different than in a normal BDSM scene. Instead of eating a piece of chocolate candy, i'm going to want to be told that he is still in love with me. i want him to tell me over coffee that my sluttiness is a good thing to him. Depending on what the scene involved, i may need to be told that he still cherishes me and wants to do it all over again.

But…more on aftercare later.

APHRODITE'S TEMPLE

The night was lit by flame and lightning bugs as we walked across the camp, twilight gray figures seen here and there as other people began a night of their own pleasures. We were heading towards a small building halfway up the hill, a dark shape that gleamed with promise from the light leaking from the windows and doorway. Unlike many of the other cabins, there was not loud music or orgiastic cries coming from that cabin – it seemed both filled with possibility and peaceful at the same time. I squeezed my husband's hand tighter as we walked, feeling a combination of love and excitement mixing deep in my belly. The whole weekend had been about sharing sacred sexuality with others, but this was going to be something more. We were heading towards something special, something even more focused on embracing that ineffable part of our sexuality.

We were going to Aphrodite's Temple.

Still holding hands, we approached the cabin, and the warm, reverent smiles of a Priest and Priestess welcomed us. As they reminded us formally of the sacred nature of this temple, they were interrupted by a loud-voiced, mostly naked drunk woman who stumbled into the torchlight. "I wanna have sexy fun god time too!" she slurred, staggering against the Priestess, who caught her with gentle, firm hands.

"I know you do, dear. And you will – but this is not the particular sexy fun god you're looking for." With a knowing glance at her partner, the priestess guided the woman away from the sacred space. Dan and I removed our shoes, bowing to the Priest as he stood at the top of the wooden steps leading to the porch. Standing at the doorway, we joined hands again as we parted the red veils.

A Priestess was waiting for us, wearing red silks draped beautifully over her voluptuous body, a theme reflected throughout the room. The cabin had been transformed by the soft warm crimson cloth circulating through the room in a sensuous flow. The reds were mingled with purples on the mattresses scattered across the floor, and more crimson and violet sashes stretched down from the ceiling, establishing the space without dividing it. It felt welcoming, enveloping. It felt for both of us a bit like coming home – a home we'd not even realized we'd been away from until we returned. I could hear my husband's breath relax, grow deeper and join with mine as we took in the feeling.

At the far end of the room an altar could be seen dimly, soft music surrounding it with a wordless, soothing melody. As our senses delighted in the wonderful mélange of sensuality, the Priestess gently directed us to dip our fingers in a small dish of water and anoint ourselves.

"This room is for getting in contact with each other as a couple. She motioned at the mattresses on the floor. "Each of these is a haven for you to shed the outside world, until only the two of you remain." She pointed again and we saw the dishes next to each one, shimmering with thick, shiny liquid. "Feel free to use the massage oil next to each haven. I wish you both joy."

Dan and I both bowed and thanked her, feeling the power of her avocation in every word she spoke and movement she made, even as she turned to greet the next couple. We turned as well, in the opposite direction, to find our own sacred haven and fulfill our rites of connection.

There were two other couples already in the room, stroking and sliding over each other, some naked, some partially dressed, all with slow, loving movements. The sexual, sensuous energy was thick in the air as we passed them, reverently, and I found myself growing heady with it as we walked on. Suddenly Dan took my hand and pulled me down to an empty mattress, a crimson drape curving down from the ceiling to pool languidly along the top edge and side. As we tumbled down, I could see the cloth rippling, sending waves up the soft cloth to the darkness above. As his body moved against mine I snuck a last glance at the other couples, seeing how their own rites rippled through the room like ours. Then I breathed out and shifted my focus to my husband.

He also wore his priest's robes, red satin, and looked unbearably sexy to me as he began to stroke and caress me. For just a moment I panicked – this was a place of slow, deliberate lovemaking, and that is just *not* my usual mode of operation. As his touch warmed my skin, though, I felt as though he were awakening new senses, a whole new nervous system coming alive under his hand. My breathing began to speed up, even more as I reached out to him and the electrical connection doubled, his skin warm and exciting under my fingers. I deepened my breathing, closed my eyes, letting the waves of passion build slowly for a change, sensing somehow that there was a power growing, growing beyond the physical stimuli.

Soon enough we were beyond the touching, kissing and feeling our bodies grow more urgent with need – but both of us knew this was not the place for that next level of intimacy. We needed to move into the next room in Aphrodite's Temple, and my body was pulsing with readiness and need.

At a soft word from Dan the Priestess came to our haven, smiling as she saw and felt our energies. As I stood up, a little shaky, she took my hand, a warm, firm grasp. Dan took my other hand and she led us to past more couples – who I'd never even heard come in – through the softly waving drapery of crimson to another entryway.

This new room was also filled with mattresses, but unlike the havens, they were configured in a very deliberate pattern. They formed a sexual ziggurat, a pyramid of soft, welcoming platforms, overlapped with soft cloths and blankets. The lowest level went along the outskirts of the wall, building layer by layer until the center rose up almost six feet off the ground. The red and purple hung from the ceiling in liquid falls of silk, shimmering in the soft, indirect light. This was a place dedicated to the practice of worshipful sex, of sacred sensual connection.

This was Aphrodite's Altar.

For a moment we simply stood there, reverently, hands clasped tight, letting the ambience of the room fill our eyes, merging the love and lust we'd built in the previous room with this more intense aura. There was no trace of the outside world in this sacred space; there was only room for the loving energy that we brought with us. Dan gave my hand a gentle tug, leading me around the edge of the pyramid, and we realized: we were the first in this room. We could choose any place we wanted to make love, to join our sex with the divine. Slowly, but inexorably, my husband led me up, bracing me against the uneven footing as we rose, level by level towards the highest point, the center of the room. He opened his arms to me there, his muscles and cock outlined by the red silk of his robes, and I felt a rush of desire and affection melting through me.

As we joined there on the highest level, it felt as though we had somehow slipped beyond the earth, into some other place outside of the realm of the real and the possible and into a place where love ruled unlimited. I knelt on the soft blankets, parting his robes enough to reveal his beautiful shaft, and took him gently in my mouth, a sacrament of pleasure given to him and taken by me at the same time. I let the taste and scent of him add to the catalog of joy filling my senses, punctuated by the sounds of his appreciation and involuntary gasps and moans. The rhythm of him sliding between my lips, our breathing, the wet slipperiness as his cock grew shiny with our mingled fluids, it all drew us deeper, into a trance-state of reverberating sex and love and lust and connected souls.

I don't know how he knew, or how I did, but at exactly the right moment Dan suddenly pushed me down onto my back, driving his cock into me with a primal urgency that was both totally different and the inevitable conclusion of the energy we'd been building. I could see that penetrating, conquering essence in his eyes and I reveled in it, my eyes locked to his, feeling his cock thicken inside of me, and I knew he was close to exploding.

"Wait for me," I gasp, begging, and he shifted expertly, maintaining his own arousal without going over the edge, drawing my own body closer and closer to climax with every driving thrust of his body grinding against me. Suddenly I was there, and he could see it in my eyes, that joyous sense of fearless abandon as we both gave ourselves over totally to the divine orgasm that shook us both in body and spirit. Our screams lifted beyond the room, beyond the cabin, to fill the night air with our joyous offering to Aphrodite.

JEALOUSY

Dan says

One story we did not include is how we ventured into the question of 'will I get jealous?' After we decided to move forward into sex that involved other people, we agreed to talk about it before and after it happened, openly and honestly, and then to do it in a nice controlled manner. More specifically, we decided that I was going to watch dawn give a man a blow job while I was nearby (not watching per se, but nearby) and then we would talk about how it felt for both of us; not just the erotic part, but the emotional part as well. That was followed by me jumping dawns bones and fucking the hell out of her while she retold me about it, but I digress.

The point is, we moved slowly, cautiously, and gave each other time to process. And we were very careful to say "I don't think I will get jealous" instead of "I won't get jealous". We are big fans of not making emotional statements like "I won't feel x" or "I'll never again feel y". Emotions are just not something to be controlled, but instead cherished and responded to.

With our blow job example above, I did not get jealous. So we kept exploring and kept pushing along. Did dawn get jealous watching me with another woman? Did she get jealous if we went to different rooms and played? Did I get jealous watching dawn beg when it was another mans cock being offered? Each one was a new experience, and each time we did our best to sit with each other and explore it.

And here is a really important part – it is ok to get jealous. Getting jealous is not a failure or a statement that you are not cut out for this. Instead, it is what you have been trained to do – get jealous – for years by society. It takes some time to untrain yourself.

The key is how you react to jealousy. We developed these two skills to help us react in a balanced way ("I am feeling pretty crappy right now about this, I need you to hold me while I have a good cry" vs "YOU FUCKING MANWHORE FROM HELL!"). First, we learned to breathe. Simple as that. Stop, take a breath. Take two. Don't tell me to calm down, but instead suggest I breath. dawn and I take this a step further and practice breathing on a daily basis (30 minutes a day of vipassana – or insight – meditation). We have found this to be a tremendous way to slow down the speed from 'something happens' to 'I reacted'. Secondly, dawn practices what she calls "Manual mode", which is where she knows her feeling are saying "scream cry hit!" and instead she sits them down and says 'Ok kids, relax a moment, have we ever been in this situation before? Did it hurt us? Did he leave us? Is this who I want to be?'

Finally, it has helped me to understand jealousy like this. Jealousy is actually rooted in what? Well, fear. Jealousy is an expression of fear. And what am I afraid of? Sharing? No. I am afraid of being abandoned, ignored, forgotten. And what is that feeling below that? Selfishness. I don't want my wife to enjoy another mans arms/cock/kisses because I am afraid there won't be enough for me. I don't want to be the kind of person that gets upset when his wife goes shoe shopping with her girlfriends because she had a good time without me. And I extend that here – I don't want to be the kind of person that gets pissy because my wife has great sex without me. I want to instead have her come home, tell me about it, and feel the joy that is in sharing her joy. "I am very happy you found the right shoes for your dress because it makes you happy. I am very happy you had your pussy eaten until the point of orgasmic release because that makes you happy."

dawn says

Dan does so well with explaining the concept of jealousy and how we both deal with it, that I don't have much to add. The only other thing that i'd like to share is that through jealousy, I found one of my root triggers, and because of this lifestyle we have chosen to embrace, this root trigger actually has the possibility of getting stepped on, frequently. To me, this is a good thing. Through authentic living, i have found a root trigger: rejection. It's not just the fear of abandonment, but rejection. It sounds like that same action, but it is really dealing with two different things. With abandonment, someone has made a choice to leave. It's all on them. With rejection, they have judged me as a person, as a being, found me unworthy and then decided to leave. It's about me.

Knowing this about myself, and about how i react to life (for whatever reason, blame it on the past or whatever), means i can use tools like 'manual mode' (slowing down for self talk) to make it through some of my moments of jealousy. This discovery about myself has been tremendously helpful in our journey forward. i want my husband to be happy in his own discoveries. The person i want to be is the wife that supports him in these journeys, as he supports me, instead of stomping her feet thinking, 'what about me?'

HARD PADDLED

April sat, shy and uncertain, alone at a small table. The bar seemed to dwarf her, the dark smoky air battered unceasingly by a jukebox that alternated between George Thorogood's raw chords and the twang of Hank Williams, Jr. She'd never heard of this place – tucked down a side street in a part of town she didn't frequent. "Jimmy's Place" was barely visible on the dirty and faded wooden sign outside, lit by single sickly yellow light.

She nursed a cola, eyes lowered, occasionally peeking up from under her long eyelashes. The person she was supposed to meet might have been there already – she wondered if he were watching her – but everyone seemed busy with their own affairs. Her nervous glances retreated anytime someone's eyes came close to making contact, riveting back to the glass in front of her. No one paid any attention, so she sat, hands wrapped around the moist glass to keep from fidgeting, her back stiff with tense anticipation. She wondered if she could go through with this; then a shift in her seat reminded her of the feeling between her legs, and she knew she had to at least try, or face a lifetime of regret for missed chances. She was past the point of turning back.

April had read the ad in the local underground paper, surreptitiously reading it at work during her break, looking for a relief from the boredom that threatened her upcoming weekend. None of the bands or local theaters interested her as she skimmed through entertainment section, and she was about to discard it when she glanced at the personals. She read them occasionally for fun, giggling at some of the possibilities the ads promised or asked for. They were obviously unreal, obviously made up by people like her with an overactive imagination.

Then she read it. And read it again, and again, and had felt the same wetness growing between her legs as she felt sitting at the table alone in the bar. It was a simple ad; someone was looking for "a submissive with an ass made for Harleys and hard paddles." April had never ridden a Harley in her life, and while the idea thrilled her, it was nothing compared to the idea of a hard wooden paddle thudding into her ass, driving down again and again, that had her heart pounding. She'd folded the paper into her pocket, wiped the sweat from her forehead, and returned to work that day. She had gone through the rest of the day in a daze, thinking of only when she would go home and find out if that ad, if that person, was for real.

At home, her fingers had trembled as she'd dialed the number, a rough masculine voice instructing her to leave a message. It was simple, direct, and not an invitation – it was an order. Voice trembling, she had managed to get out "This is April…" and then had stammered out her phone number before slamming down the phone and hugging her knees to her chest. She had actually called! Her body had started shaking uncontrollably, and she couldn't tell If it was for fear that the deep voice would call back or that he wouldn't. She had settled into an agony of waiting and fantasizing and anticipating, only half-aware of the fantasy that she was trying to make come true.

Two days later there had been a message on her answering machine. She'd pushed the "play" button with her heart pounding, and let out a small cry at the husky voice that growled out of the tiny speaker. Matter-of-factly it told her what to wear, clothing and makeup, and where to go and when. Then he had told her what was expected. "When you get here, you will do as you're told. You will be safe, but you will be pushed beyond any fantasy you've ever had. You have my word on both those counts."

Hearing the confident assurance in his voice had filled April with a thrilling terror, a hunger for the power it promised. She'd dated men looking for it, but never found it; instead it had fueled the fantasies as she touched herself at night. That kind of voice; those kinds of words. There was no question of backing out. She would wear those clothes, she would put on that makeup, and she would get that hard paddling.

Now she sipped her drink, wearing the clothes he'd asked her to wear in the unfamiliar bar where he'd told her to come. She knew he'd know what she looked like – she was the only one dressed this way – but she had no idea who he might be. That voice could have belonged to any of the men here, or to any of the strong images she'd conjured up while masturbating. April fidgeted impatiently, desperately wanting to meet the real him, to resolve that cloud of uncertainty. Every time the door at the front of the bar opened, she would peek up, trying to catch a glimpse of the patron, heart thudding because it might be the real him. But the men just walked to the bar, ordered their drink and then swaggered back to the noisy activity by the pool tables, loudly greeting their friends with handshakes and pats on the back.

April's nervousness ratcheted up a notch. She was feeling, more and more, that while no one was meeting her gaze…there were still whispers, glances, knowing nods towards her table that she almost caught out of the corner of her eye. No one approached the table, no one so much as looked her way – and that's when it hit her. A single woman, alone in a bar full of men, and no one so much as offers to buy her a drink? Suddenly she was filled with doubt – this was obviously the wrong bar, how stupid could she be, this was a joke, a cruel prank. The guy was nothing more than a voice, a good ol' boy enjoying a laugh with his friends to see just how long this dumb bimbo would sit there waiting for the nonexistent man to match the words on her answering machine. She was nothing but a silly girl, she realized, frustrated and angry with herself at being duped, at actually hoping this would be anything more. Then the anger gave way to resignation, disappointment, and she sighed, rising from her seat.

At that moment the door opened – and the bar went silent. She looked up – and saw the real him.

His shaven head topped a thickly built frame, filling the doorway with an aura of height that went beyond mere physicality before he strode into the room. He wore biker leathers, their worn black dulled a bit by road dust but obviously well-kept. His boots thudded on the floor, somehow filling her ears beyond the sound of the steel guitar on the juke, and he walked directly to her. There was no question in his eyes or manner. He knew who she was, and what she was there for. She couldn't take her eyes off of him as he approached, even though she knew everyone else was watching. Without looking down he grabbed a chair, twirled it around and straddled it, moving with an easy, confident grace. "April," he acknowledged her with a slight incline of his head, and she nodded in response, heart beating too loudly to allow her a voice.

"Are you ready? This is your only chance to back out." His voice was even more resonant and husky in person.

April wanted to pour out her fantasies, tell him of the thousand ways she'd imagined him taking her, tell him of the years she'd spent with lover after lover trying to fill this need but never succeeding. Her mouth was dry as her mind raced, and she managed only "I...I've been waiting for this." Her voice shook, but only a little.

His gaze never left hers, even as he addressed the room. "Joey. Lock the door."

Joey was a young man that she'd noticed before with a high-and-tight haircut and rippling smooth muscles, He moved quickly to the door with a clear "Sure thing, Spade, Sir," Even as April wondered at the "Sir" she was struck by the fact that the younger man was also dressed in leathers – pants, a tight shirt, and a dog collar around his neck. As Joey locked the door and flipped over the *Sorry, we're closed!* Sign, he turned and April say the gleeful look on his face as he watched her and Spade.

April's pussy felt like a river now, as she stood there trembling before Spade's commanding gaze. She rubbed them together slightly, reveling in the slickness there even as her stomach turned circles. She let her eyes close, trying to calm down, to breathe – then her eyes snapped open as he barked out "April!"

She looked at him, standing there, his arms – those strong, enveloping arms – stretched wide to either side. "Is this what you expected, April?"

She swallowed, hard, then mutely shook her head.

"Speak, girl!"

"No sir this isn't what I expected at all," the words came out of her in a rush, as if his command had somehow unlocked it. She flicked her eyes left and right, seeing the many men gathered around, all watching her. "Aren't we...going somewhere private?" she asked, her voice a tiny sound lost in the crowd, barely a whisper.

Spade rose from his chair, a cruel smile shaping his lips. "Oh, no,little Missy," he said. "I share my toys with my friends." Approaching her around the table, he leaned down and put his hands on her thighs, his grip tight but not painful. He bent to her ear, and she felt his breath like fire as he whispered "Isn't this what you want? Aren't you all juicy and wet for me?"

"Oh," she whispered again, unable to move. "Oh, yes, sir."

At her answer, he took her by surprise, grabbing her hair and pulling her up. With a shocked squeal she tried to follow where he led, stumbling across the floor to the pool table. She let out a whoosh of air as he bent her over it, pushing her face down and to the side so that her cheek mashed into the stained green felt. His fingers were tightly tangled in her hair, forcing her head down harder, and she felt his other hand grabbing her ass as he kicked her feet apart. She could hear the other men cheering, hooting, clinking their glasses together as they jostled closer to the pool table trying to get a better view of what Spade was doing. She closed her eyes, trying to escape the delicious wave of embarrassment that coursed through her, and then opened them wide in shock as Spade yanked the back of her skirt high up over her ass cheeks. She could feel the air cooling the slick wetness that covered her thighs. Reflexively her hands moved to pull it back down, and Spade absently slaps them away, growling his displeasure. That was enough for her to drop them, surrendering in a mixture of desire, shock, and shame.

Spade leisurely ran his coarse hands over her firm smooth curves that lay exposed before him. "Such a good girl, doing what you're told," he drawled out. "No panties to get in my way." He gave her left cheek a hard pinch and then pulled her arms up, one after another, behind her back, never loosening his grip on her hair. "Anybody want to donate their bandana?" he asked the crowd, and instantly a flurry of colors erupted from the denim pockets as the men dug in. Spade grabbed the closest one, a gray fabric, and used it to tie her wrists tightly behind her back. He finally released her hair even as he kicked her feet even further apart, and before she could regain her balance he pulled her skirt even higher, up and over her bound arms until the tangle of loose cloth was around her head, covering her face in the soft fabric that smelled of her sex. Her ass felt vulnerable, as exposed as her face was hidden, and she felt a thrill of objectification at the wantonness of it, feeling the stares of the men around her.

Spade pulled her upright,roughly, and quickly lifted her breast out past the neckline of her shirt. She heard the men murmur in approval and lust as her nipple hardened under their gaze, but she only listened for his approval, feeling herself automatically lifting as he reached for the other. When both nipples were exposed he pushed her back down over the pool table, dragging them across the dark green cloth until they burned with sensation. She moaned, and heard him chuckle, turning her voice into a gasping cry as his fingers suddenly thrust between her legs. She felt him spread her lips, pushing their swollen wetness wide as he drew his finger slowly, inexorably from her clit to her ass. April's knees buckled and she moaned louder as she fought to stay upright.

"Oh, yes, this is a good one, guys," Spade said. "Slick and ready."

He pulled the skirt away from her face and lifted her head, looking into her eyes. She looked back at him, conflicting waves of passion and frustration seeming to battle for control. He watched her for what seemed an eternity, and she felt measured, weighed, evaluated. *He wants to know if I'm really into it,* she realized, and though she was beyond words, she tried to show with her eyes, her mouth, her body that yes, this was joy, this was rapture, this was the kink she needed. To give her ass to him tonight, for the hard paddle.

Seeming satisfied, he released her head, and she fell back to the table, her neck sore and stiff. She could feel her face flushed with heat while at the same time her ass was covered with goose bumps, and she shivered slightly. The moment of connection had given her some measure of confidence, and she began to move beyond the shock of his exposure of her skin. April realized that this was *exactly* what she wanted, and she began to revel in it. She found herself hoping for him to keep pushing her, to continue this "play" until it was more than she could handle. Her ass wiggled a bit at the thought, and she jumped with a yip of pain as Spade's hand came down hard on the left cheek, the resounding *thwack* reverberating through her skull and sending echoes of pleasure through her clit and nipples. She moaned and arched her back, rubbing her nipples harder against the pool table, desperate suddenly for more sensation.

Her eyes closed tightly, focusing on the feeling, the amazing waves of warmth spreading through her, starting from the spot where Spade's hand had come down. She knew the men could see her, and she loved it, but she squeezed her eyes shut anyway, focusing on her body. This was better than any fantasy, better than any masturbation. She felt his hand again on her ass, this time rubbing the welt almost thoughtfully before he lifted her head again slightly. She opened her eyes and looked at him steadily, almost daringly. A slight smile curved his mouth, and he released her again.

Smacking her ass almost absently, he called out "Hey, Johnny. Come and warm this ass up for me. You need the practice." Instantly her calm evaporated, and she realized that had been the eye of the hurricane. She heard the young man's boots on the floor behind her, close, and then felt his rough denim jeans pressing into her ass as he pressed his crotch between her spread legs. She could feel the hot bulge of his cock through the jeans, pressing into her left thigh. *He must be enjoying the show,* she thought as the steel-hard erection pushed against her. Then Johnny stepped back, letting his hands brush her ass cheeks almost gently, stroking them, warming them against the air…and then he began tapping her skin.

Soft taps, at first, gradually getting harder, but never even approaching the level of spanking that April craved. Then, as he continued, she noticed that they were getting worse – not because of the intensity, but because he was tap-tap-tapping in the same spot, on each cheek, and the repeated sensation built up inside of her, until she was writhing, stretching up on her toes and arching her back trying to bring the sensation up beyond that threshold of teasing pleasure. But Johnny adjusted his strikes, never varying, never allowing her to increase or decrease her own sensation, as he built up the heat at his own pace. She moaned, and Johnny shifted to the side, his hand pressing at the small of her back as he raised the intensity even more, his hand falling in a rhythmic *smack-smack* over and over. April's cheeks felt molten, and she wondered if they glowed as red as they felt.

Finally Spade stepped in, slapping Johnny on the back and letting him step away. Looking at April's ass, he commented "You don't need as much practice as I thought, boy. Good job." Then he reached out and tangled his fingers in her hair again, pulling her face up off the table. Leaning in, again she felt his hot breath on her ear. "How do you feel now, April?"

Her voice shook, but she managed to answer promptly. "On fire and in heaven, Sir!"

"That's good, slut. We've only just started. I think it's time to step it up a bit."

"Step it...up, sir?" she gasped, nervously.

"Oh, yes," he replied with a growling chuckle. "You didn't think *that* was a hard paddling, did you? Little Joey was just an appetizer. A warm-up for that fine ass of yours. Unless – " His eyes drove into her, and she felt as if the power of his gaze was stealing her breath. "Unless that's all your little slut-girl fantasy can take. Give the word, April, and it all stops. Right now, this instant. You got a nice little spanking from a hot leatherboy, that's enough to go home and masturbate to, right? End of story." April felt tears beginning to gather in her eyes as he spoke of ending, and she knew he saw, because he smiled. "Of course, if you did that, it would be a final decision. You'd never be allowed back." He released her hair, and her head sank to the green felt, the fabric darkening as the tears met the surface. "Make a choice, April."

She was quiet for a moment. She knew the thought of continuing this should terrify her, horrify her, that she should get up and run for the door and a safe, normal life.

But this feeling – exposed, naked, bound before these dark men with their motorcycles and leathers and hands and denim and boots and *him* – Sir Spade. She felt alive, she felt an amazing freedom at the thought of giving herself no way out. *No way out.* Just the thought made the juices drip down her thighs, and her nipples tightened into hard little pebbles. The tears that fell under her face were not of fear or pain – they were of joy, the joy of finally, *finally* being exactly where she wanted to be. She had dreamed of this exact moment, and had never thought it would happen.

She was resolved. Taking a breath, decision made, she spoke, loud and clear as a bell in the smoky room.

"Please, sir. Please spank me. Please…take me!" She wiggled her ass, lewd and wanton, and not caring. She was his.

Spade laughed out loud, delighted at her submission. "That's what I like to hear!" He slapped her wiggling cheeks, and she lifted them higher, to please him. "We've found ourselves a real slut here, boys. Let's give her what she wants!"

Spade pulled her up from the table, letting her skirt fall loosely back around her hips, covering her legs. April wondered at that – *Doesn't he want me naked?* Then all thoughts fled her mind as he pulled a knife from his belt and flipped it open with a loud click. Before she could scream, the blade flashed out, slicing through the fabric under her breasts, left, right, up, down, until it is just rags and tatters vainly trying to cover the warm flesh of her breasts and belly.

Then it was time for the skirt – the blade coming down inside the waistband, making her afraid to move (as if she could move anyway) as Spade sliced it, just a bit. Then his hands reached out and violently ripped it apart with a sound that matched the ragged hoarseness of her breathing. He also tore away the remains of the shirt, and she stood naked before him and the rest of the men. This time, though, she was not timid; instead of trying to shield herself, she arched her back, throwing her arms back, thrusting out her breasts proudly. She was rewarded by applause from a few of the men, though their smiles looked more predatory than friendly.

Spade twirled his chair closer to her, sitting down in front of her, his strong hands resting on his thighs as he looked at her, eye-level with her areolae, answering her smile with a hard grin. Reaching up, he twisted her nipple harshly, drawing her down and across his lap, the rough denim feeling wondrous against her skin. As he shifted his legs slightly, April gave a tiny yelp. Her legs were off the floor, and for a dizzying moment it felt as though she would fall. Spade's hands were sure, though, and as one held her fast to his lap the other traced a line gently down the sloping curve of her back. As his hand reached the small of her spine, he lifted it ceremoniously and brought it down with a *whack!* on her ass.

"Ouch!" April squealed. "That hurts!" Her voice sounded offended, filled with wounded pride, as if he'd been discourteous at a formal dinner. Her hands, though, tried to reach back and cover her cheeks before he could strike again, but she was far too slow. *Whack!* April's body almost rebounded off his strong thighs as he spanked her, rubbing her ass again in between the blows. The next time his hand came down, the blow sent a tingling wave through her body. She tried to relax, to focus on and enjoy that sensation. *Maybe this won't be bad at all,* she dared to think, letting another wave of pleasure wash through her as Spade spanked her again.

Though she couldn't see his face, April felt she knew what Spade looked like at that moment, in his element, with the object of his fetish, her cherry-red ass under his hand. She can feel every gnarl and callous of his hand as her skin grows more tender, swelling pink and raw with each strike. She can even feel his hardness growing under her belly, and the thought of it makes her moan, the sound turning into a breathy wail as his hand comes down again. She doesn't want to relax any more – her body writhes on his lap, crazy with sensation, with desire, with the burning that travels from her ass through her very soul. A small part of her mind wonders idly, through the haze of lust, if she'll ever sit again. But the hand comes down again and drives all thought from her mind.

Then he suddenly stops, his own breath harsh with exertion, and moves his knees in a way that somehow tells April she should stand. She manages to get upright, somewhat shakily, her eyes trying to focus on this man that has mastered her. She can make out that he is smiling, grinning widely, and something inside of her sings with accomplishment. She had pleased him…now she just had to stay balanced on legs that felt like they would give way under her burning, burning ass.

"Kneel, slut," Spade commanded, and April found that her legs worked perfectly well. She sank down before him without hesitation.

He looked into the open expectant expression on her face, and rose from the chair, letting his crotch press into her face. Again she felt his hardness pressing through the leather, and impulsively she flicked out her tongue, wanting a taste of that granite muskiness. Spade yanked her head back, growling. "That's not what you're here for. If you are a good girl. I may let you beg for it later." With a dismissive flick he released her head, and she rocked on her knees, shaken.

He left her there, kneeling naked on the floor, head bowed, as he walked around, drink in hand. He chatted with his buddies, his loud bass laugh punctuating the steady murmurs of conversation that filled the bar. April tried to sit a bit more comfortably, shifting her ass from her heels to her calves and back, but she was unable to find a comfortable position. She kept her head bowed, and concentrated on bearing the pain for him. Her skin still burned deliciously red-hot where his hand had come down.

Suddenly he was back again, standing before her, and she cried out as he again tangled his fingers in her hair and lifted her unceremoniously to her feet. He quickly led her back to the pool table, so quickly that she *whuffed* over as her waist hit the edge, her face again pressing down into the green felt still damp from her tears. Then she felt a delicious coolness soothe the fiery skin of her ass. Spade was running his cold beer back and forth across the curve of her ass, and she swayed from side to side with the pleasure of it. Her nipples were hard again, and her whole body was covered with goosebumps. April felt like she was in heaven, until the bottle was suddenly taken away, her ass returning with a vengeance to that spicy pain that made it seem to glow. She waggled her hips slightly, longing for Spade to bring the bottle back, but he simply gave her a swat in return. "Be still," he commanded, and walked away from her.

April turned her head up slightly from the table, watching him walk, the whole world canted ninety degrees in her vision. Somehow that seemed right, too, her whole world had changed, pain was pleasure, vulnerability was secure, why shouldn't sideways be up? She saw him reach behind the bar, his hand coming up with one paddle, then another. Suddenly she was trembling again, and was grateful for the solidity of the table because she knew her legs would not have held her up. *This is what I came here for,* she thought, realizing that everything else had been a warm up.

Spade saw her watching as he sauntered over to her, and he held up one of the paddles. "Is this what you want? Is this what you're craving? Tell me, slut, is this what you need?"

April couldn't seem to find a voice, and she nodded, her tears falling again to the felt under her cheek.

"I want you to say it, April."

Swallowing, she licked her lips, and tried again. "Yes, sir. Please. Please…paddle me." She swallowed again. "Please take me to a place I've never been before."

Spade straightened up, satisfied. "Men. Put her in position."

She heard the men scrambling around her, felt their hands reach out and grab her tightly, but she couldn't take her eyes off of Spade. He moved again to the back of the bar, bringing out a sawhorse from a doorway marked "Employees Only." The horse was more than just wood – leather and padding had been tacked to it securely, and it had become a piece of furniture with one obvious purpose: spanking. The men pulled her over to it, and she cooperated as they lay her down lengthwise, the soft texture of leather hitting between her legs and making her gasp before she was pushed forward, feeling it press along her belly, her chest, her breasts hanging down alongside, making her feel almost like an animal being prepared for sacrifice. The bandana was untied and she felt a sweet ache in her shoulders as her arms released down. Someone brought out handcuffs and she felt the unyielding steel snap shut over each wrist, cold and harshly contrasting with the soft bandana. Two more sets of handcuffs fastened her ankles to the legs of the bench, with leather straps added to her thighs. She began to panic a bit as another leather strap was suddenly laid across the small of her back, tightening just short of breathlessness. She couldn't move, couldn't so much as wiggle, and as a blindfold she opened her mouth to scream – but was denied even that when someone shoved the bandana into her mouth, gagging her, another wrapped and tied securely around the back of her head so that she couldn't spit it out.

As April tested her bonds, first gingerly, then more and more frantically, her mind raced. *Oh, Shit, Oh, Shit, Oh, Shit, Oh, Shit,* she thought, *What have I gotten myself into?* She felt a part of herself want to panic, but somehow the greater part of herself accepted her place here. There was a strange security to being strapped down so tightly that she couldn't move, blindfolded so she couldn't see what was coming, gagged so she couldn't protest. She could still here the murmur of voices, the clink of glasses, but there was a kind of peaceful stillness to her mind, an open, expectant waiting, combining the burning pain of her ass with the throb of desire still in her dripping pussy.

She felt someone – Spade? She couldn't even be sure – come up behind her, the rough denim of his pants rubbing against her exposed pussy. She trembled at the pressure, feeling the surge of wetness, the hot flush of blood engorging her lips, and suddenly she was filled with the trembling need for him – whoever it was – to fuck her and spank her and just take her. Then she felt a hand along her thigh, fingers stroking up towards her pussy, and she knew it was Spade, the memory of that same hand still burnt into the skin of her ass. Even bound as she was, she strained to arch, push up, move herself closer to his hand, to show how eager she was for his touch. Spade let his fingers slide tantalizingly close to her eager and dripping vulva, wide and exposed – but instead of rewarding her need, he bypassed it, stroking the other leg, and chuckling softly at the frustrated whimper it caused her.

"You want me to fill you up, slut?" he asked with a low rumble that sank thru her. Unable to respond verbally, she bobbed her head up and down, a desperately affirmative *yes yes yes!*

The she felt that cold smooth sensation return, a solid curving object following the trail blazed by his fingers moments before. At first it felt good, cooling the fiery pain of her spanking. Then as Spade continued to roll the bottle along her thighs, he let it slide nearer and nearer her cunt. *Not what I meant!* She screamed with need silently inside the darkness of the gag and blindfold, both loving and hating the sensation of her pussy being filled with the hard unyielding bottle. Aloud she couldn't do more than moan as it sank in deeper and deeper, the cold condensation of the bottle mingling with her own juices to let it slide easily within her. She felt unbelievably dirty as the sheer unreality of being fucked by a beer bottle sent her over the edge. *Naughty girl, his dirty naughty girl,* she thought as her body took over and she began to grind and fuck the contoured glass.

When she felt it withdrawn the emptiness of her pussy was like an ache, but before she could protest she was filled again, this time with a softer, more pliant object, one she knew well from her own masturbation. The thick silicone dildo stretched her wide, wider, bigger than anything she'd ever even fantasized about, and her mouth widened as she tried to gasp around the gag, making wet slurping noises as she drooled and moaned simultaneously. Dimly she was conscious of hearing a man's voice say "God *damn,* look at her take all of it!" and she felt another surge of wanton freedom, knowing she was Spade's dirty little slut on display. The thought made her even hornier, and she felt her pussy get even wetter as the dildo slid in and out of her.

All thoughts of the dildo were forgotten as the first strike of the paddle slammed into her ass. She tried to scream but the breath was caught by the second *whack* and she realized there was no way to prepare, no way to react, she simply had to lie there spread before him and take his hard paddling. *This is what I came here for,* she thought, as strike after strike comes down. There is no finesse to this, no variation – Spade simply gave her what he promised, a paddling without mercy, each strike as hard as the last, no need for ramping up because they are all just *hard.* April's head felt light, her body almost insensate except for the burning of her skin under the thick wood Spade was using, but then her pussy felt the dildo move inside of her. Somehow Spade was not only paddling her hard but also fucking her, the dildo sliding in and out easily, warm from her body heat. As the pleasure and pain mingled, she felt that she might pass out, her ass moving back to take more of the strikes, to drive the dildo in further. There was no thought in her mind save the need for harder fucking, harder paddling, her entire body turned into a massive craving need for *more. Harder. Deeper. Please.*

The paddling stopped then for a moment, though the movement of the dildo in and out of her pussy continued. She let out a whimpering, insatiable sound of need as Spade removed the gag from her mouth. "Had enough, slut?"

"*NO Sir!*" her voice sounds strange even to her, desperate and pleading. "More, sir, I need more! I want to be fucked and spanked and used for you, by you, anything for you, sir, please don't stop!" She knew she was babbling but she didn't care – the fucking was driving her mad with the need to cum, and somehow she knew that the paddle would have to come down again, unmercifully and beautifully savage, in order for that to happen.

Spade let out a chuckle and dropped the gag on the floor, letting the room fill with the sound of her guttural moans as the dildo continues its inexorable pumping into her cunt. He picked up the paddle and raised it high, bringing it down with a sharp wet *crack* of wood on flesh, again and again. April could almost feel the way he smiled as the sounds she made changed, deliciously mingling the pleasure and pain. Though she couldn't see it, somehow she knew his cock was hard as a baseball bat, too, as was every other cock in the room. *They all want to fuck me,* she thought, and let her cries get louder and even more slutty. "Cock!" she gasps out. "Please, I need a cock in me. Mouth, pussy, just fuck me, please, I can't stand it, I need cock!"

Spade simply grunted in assent, and suddenly April heard the simultaneous approach of two pairs of boots along with the rasp of zippers being pulled down. She opened her mouth just in time to feel the delicious tickle of a warm cock sliding along the roof of her mouth, and she opened wider to take it down into her throat. She felt a burst of pride as she heard the man moan, and she began sucking, bobbing her head. Then it was her turn to cry out as the silicone dildo was finally taken out of her pussy and the slick condom-covered cock rammed into her vulva from behind. The men took her the same way Spade was paddling her – hard, remorseless stokes, her face mashed into the denim of the man in front of her with every thrust. She could feel the man behind her grab her hips, pulling himself harder into her. *Yes, fuck me!* she thought, suddenly realizing that the paddling had stopped. Somehow her ass felt simultaneously relieved and needy, craving another blow even as the skin screamed with burning fire.

She felt Spade's hand again, then, on her back, as if measuring, evaluating the slick sheen of perspiration that covered her skin as the men roughly fucked her. Then there was a hissing snap and a new band of fiery sensation lit across her back, like a dragon's tongue, again and again criss-crossing her skin as Spade whipped her. As the leather bit into her skin she could feel the welts lifting, and knew she would wear his mark for weeks after. April's eyes teared up with gratitude as she gave herself up to the pain of the whip and the joy of the fucking.

Suddenly the man in front of her growls, mashing her face flat into his pelvis as he fills her throat with his hot cum. Eagerly April swallowed, wanting to suck him dry, to show Spade what a good cock slut she was, and as he finally pulled his cock free of her lips she had a swollen pout, not wanting to let go. Then she gurgled in surprise and delight as another cock pushes into her mouth and the rhythm starts again. Behind her comes another roar as the unknown biker thrusts his own orgasm deep within her, and for just a moment her pussy is empty – then, as she hoped, another cock, this one slightly thicker, drives into her. New hands grab her hips, and she surrendered to the motion, the sensation, the sheer objectification of being Spade's fucktoy gift to his friends. Her screams were muffled by the cock in her mouth as a confluence of his whip across her shoulder blades and the man behind her slamming into her bruised ass finally drove her over the edge and she came.

Once she started, it seemed she would never stop, waves of orgasm coursing through her as she shuddered, feeling her body explode again and again as cock after cock took her mouth and cunt. April's cries grew softer as her body seemed to float, suspended on cocks and driven by the sting of the whip, a strange state of blissful lust filling her mind. She could feel Spade's presence through it all, his whip expertly covering her back and shoulders with the ecstasy of the thousand cuts he delivered, occasionally stroking a welt with the now-familiar rough calluses on his fingers.

Finally the last man spent into her mouth, and she reflexively swallowed and opened her mouth for the next – but there was no one to take her, she had sated them all, and through the painful welts and delicious soreness of her pussy and jaw she felt a strange sense of pride. *They took me, and I took them,* she thought dazedly. *I took them for him.*

Spade uncuffed her and lifted her up, not gently but with a precision that bespoke his satisfaction with her performance. His hand encircled the back of her neck and he slowly drew her to him, letting her face press into the soft leather of his vest. She breathe in the secure scent of him, feeling utterly safe and exactly where she belonged. After a moment her eyes opened, and April shyly drew away from Spade and looked around the room. Men lounged about as before, some with their semi-erect cock still hanging out of their jeans, cigarettes and beers in their hands as though the entire scene was a routine event. No one seemed to pay her any more attention than when she'd first come in and sat at the table.

No one but Spade.

He lifted her chin up, the rough skin of his hands feeling warm against her face. His other arm went around her shoulders possessively.

"Ever ridden a Harley before?" Spade asked her, his eyes bright like a hunter who has captured his prey.

"No, sir," April whispered, not able to move, not wanting to, ever.

"Well, it's about time you tried." Spade lifted his jacket from the chair next to them. "Here. Put this on. But make sure that bare bruised ass of yours is on my seat, and you'd best press those tits into me hard enough that I can feel your nipples. That clear?"

"Yes, sir," April said, a little louder, her voice more steady as she was enveloped in his leathers.

"Let's go, slut." As Spade led her out the door, April reflexively felt a pang of concern at her nakedness, but it was replaced by a sense of pride. She wanted people to see what she was, what she'd done for him.

She straddled the bike behind him, reveling in dull ache of her hard paddled ass on the leather seat, and pressed into Spade's back as the bike roared out of the parking lot and into the dawn.

GROUP SEX

Dan says

Group sex can be the fulfillment of many fantasies. It can also be scary, a logistical nightmare, messy, and emotionally triggering (thinks like abandonment issues and jealousy, which we talk about elsewhere in this book). It can even be boring!

Now, don't take this as a negative at all. Many of the stories in this book include group sex in different forms and it really can be pretty terrific. But it helps to consider some things before you get started.

Finding people can be tricky. Swing clubs and play parties help – people who go there are often attending for sex after all. And many a website can assist you as well (much more likely to start talking to people, much less likely to actually physically meet with them). But even as slutty and naughty and visible as dawn and I are, we go long times between meeting people. Part of that is because we are picky, part of that is because we…ok, the other part is because we are picky as well. If I want dawn to go get boned tonight, I can take her to a club, tie her up, put a box of condoms on her ass and say "Help yourself" and she will get a dick put in her. But we are actually looking for something else (today, although once dawn reads this part, I expect a "can we can we can we").

If you meet and engage with people you know, that can be great – but also has a different wrinkle. If you and your spouse decide to hook up with the neighbor and his wife, great! But if it doesn't go well…they still live there, you still live here…. and can get complicated. Same of course for having your boss over to the house and you and the Mrs. tag teaming her, or your best friend takes on the role of the plumber in a fantasy. There is less fear because it is someone you know, but a new kind of fear takes its place.

The other big deal to talk about – and you really do need to talk about it – is sexually transmitted infections. STI's (or sometimes called STD's, sexually transmitted diseases) are something that should not be ignored. As you can tell in this book, dawn and I have not followed the only way of complete avoidance of STI's (which is abstinence) but we talked to each other and decided what safer sex routines makes most sense for us.

Will you use condoms for all penetration? Will you only play with a certain group of people and seek to be fluid bonded to them (fluid bonding is the concept of you don't use protection, but you only have sex with mutually agreed partners, and they don't have sex outside your circle either)? Will you use safer sex for oral sex as well? This is a big one if you go to swing clubs. Everyone is fine with condoms, but few know what a dental dam (used like a condom but for oral sex with women) is.

You and your partner will need to do some research. Get the facts from more than one source. Realize that you can protect yourself as much as possible, but not 100% (condoms break). And decide what is acceptable risk.

dawn says

Actually, group sex is one of those naughty fantasies that we get to turn into reality every now and then – but as Dan said, it can be hard for us to find partners. Because of this, i have a couple of fantasies in the group sex realm that haven't been fulfilled after all of these years. i'm ok with that. Once you've lived out all of your fantasies, what's left? But, if i had a chance to live out those two fantasies tonight, i would certainly think hard about following through. It's not the fear that stops me any more like it might have been in the past. It is something else entirely.

Pickiness – Dan hit the nail on the head. i want a certain feeling when i play with someone. It's not about the action itself; nor how the other person looks, or anything like that; it's about the connection with the other person as we engage in some naughty action. i must admit though, one reason that some of my 'fantasies turned to reality' work, is because Dan is there with me. If i don't have a connection to the person that we've involved in our play, at least i have a connection with Dan. i'm able to let out my slutty side at that point and that creates a smaller connection with the other person, but still a connection. Without that connection, it won't work.

i caught myself today thinking of a naughty scene that i'd like to play out and realized that it wouldn't work without a certain feeling involved. i actually felt a little disappointed that i can't just put an ad out there anymore looking for someone that would perform a certain action with me. Today, i could be fucked by a roomful of guys, but if that feeling isn't there, if that place of vulnerability and sluttiness isn't there, then it's just cocks and pussy doing an action. That understanding of myself, does make things a little difficult when it comes to putting these fantasies together.

i will keep trying though. i have fantasies that i plan on fulfilling, even if it takes years. Until then, i plan on enjoy this slutty trip as it presents itself!

OBJECTIFICATION ROOM

Our vacation could have been a typical one for campers – my husband and I being no stranger to the outdoors. The campsite had the typical large dining hall of "family" campgrounds, with long wooden tables and cafeteria food and knots of other campers laughing and eating in various groups. It could have been a scene out of *Dirty Dancing*, right up to the "list of events" on the wall and on the program that my husband and I were huddled over, looking at the list of activities. We were trying to plan our day – our week, really – and the available options were …intriguing, to say the least.

This wasn't your typical family campground – unless you were talking about a leather family. And the activities, while wide-ranging, were definitely adult, pansexual, and kink-friendly – just like the camp itself. That suited my husband and me just fine – we just had to actually *pick* from all the things that we wanted to do.

One weekend event that really intrigued me was called "The Objectification Room." The blurb about it was sexy and tantalizing but a bit short on detail. He saw what I was looking at, and grinned.

"You think?" he asked, in that shorthand speak that you fall into after years of marriage.

I answered in kind. "Dunno... Voyeur, maybe. More, if I like it, next time around." I didn't really have a clear idea of what the room was about. "Objectification" – usually that meant people treated as, well, objects. But what did that really mean? Tables, chairs, footstools, lamps? But I'd heard people talking about the room and they kept breaking into giggle fits, so I thought maybe I was wrong. "Worth a look, at least." My husband trumped the verbal shorthand game by grunting assent, and we went on to look at other options.

I didn't expect to think about it much as the week went on, with so many other fun activities – but we kept hearing snippets about it here and there, inside jokes between new friends we made, little mentions of things that would be done with the "objects" in the room. Frustratingly, though, they would never quite be clear what the room was about and by the end of the week, I really had no better idea of what I was going to see in the Objectification Room than when I'd first read about it.

The curiosity peaked in the shower one evening with my husband, when he suddenly said, "About the Objectification room...I think you ought to do more than watch. You should participate."

"Huh?" I said, pretending to be surprised. "Why would you say that?" We both knew the answer to that, though, and he just looked at me and I blushed, glancing down at the soapy water at my feet. He and I had both shared my fantasies of being used in that way, of being objectified, reduced to a material, sensual *thing*. But I hadn't allowed myself to think about participating in something so...intense. Especially, since it was our first experience at a big event like this.

The thought wouldn't go away, though. I looked online at pictures from last year. I read the description again and again, trying to wrap my mind around it. I even asked a friend, Fyre, who'd been there last year, to tell me about her experience there, and as she spun out a tale of what she'd witnessed I could feel my inner slut sit up and take notice. By the time she was done, I was wet and squirmy and had butterflies in my stomach. I thanked her, and as she walked away, I knew: I had to try it. I couldn't try it. Could I? Maybe…no. It was too much. Too intense. Too extreme. It was the kind of thing the swingers and nymphos did. That wasn't me. Was it?

Saturday morning came, and my husband and I went to the workshop that was going to explain the things that would happen that night throughout the camp. The event was amazingly thorough in catering to everyone's pansexuality – there would be a room of "prostitution", an orgy room, glory holes…and the Objectification Room. That one they described last, as if sadistically savoring my own burning curiosity. In reality, it was pride of place, because this was the presenter's baby – they'd invented this idea themselves. The goal was to provide a safe place for people to live out their fantasies of anonymous sex. As they described it, I found myself unconsciously grinding on my chair and squeezing my mate's hand so tight that he chuckled. I growled at him and his amusement at my excitement at the concept of actually following through with… whatever this would be.

"Here's the details," the presenter said, her grin like the pride of a parent showing off a particularly bright child. "The Objectification Room is a cabin that has five single beds in it. There's a veil hanging down from the ceiling in such a way that the upper half of the beds are blocked from view." She paused, looking over the crowd at us, and her smile grew wider, as if she was imagining me – us – or maybe that was just my own projecting.

"The 'objects' will lay nude on the beds with just their lower half exposed. The veil will block the upper half of their bodies from being seen or touched at all." There were some murmurs of protest from boob enthusiasts in the room, but they were quickly hushed by the rest of us who were entranced by the…possibilities. "There will be a sign on the veil, over the 'objects', saying what you can and can't do. At the voyeur side of the room the guard – er, I mean, monitor – " there was a titter of amusement at the slip; the presenter was well known for her prisoner fantasies – "will make sure that everyone uses safer sex techniques. Condoms, lube, gloves, dental dams, you know the drill. They are also there to answer any questions from those watching and those…waiting." She seemed to be looking directly at me, suddenly. "There's also a monitor behind the veil that will take care of the objects. Each one will have a bell they can ring if they need anything. They will be…well-maintained." That laid one of my fears to rest. Like any sexually aware adult, especially one with a committed partner, safety was paramount in my reality, even if it wasn't in my fantasies. And here was a fantasy that I'd always thought would be out of reach, with all the little details covered, being handed to me. How could I pass it up? I glanced at my husband, and saw his eyes sparkling with eagerness. He was turned on by the idea; I was practically sitting in a puddle just from the description. Suddenly the decision was made.

I went to the presenter and asked if there was still a need for "objects." She smiled, and I realized that she had seen my reaction during her presentation. "A lot of people have expressed interest," she said, sounding regretful. She must have seen my crestfallen expression, because she reached out and patted my arm. Her touch felt electric in my wound-up state, and I jumped a little. Her teeth flashed as she smiled wider. "Tell you what. I won't really have things set until 9:30. The room opens at 10pm. Come a little early… and we'll see."

For the rest of the day I was a woman obsessed. I asked everyone what they thought of the Objectification Room. I badgered my husband, expressing concerns, nervously talking about my doubts about anonymous people taking pleasure from my body even while he could see that I was completely turned on by it. At 7pm I garnered enough courage to actually go and find the people setting up the room, and after being passed around from helper to helper, finally got to the person in charge of taking in volunteers for "objects".

His manner was brusque, not in an unfriendly way, just in the manner of someone who was busy. "Wanna volunteer? Cool. Here's the sign, here's a marker. Just write down your limits."

He was about to turn away, and I spluttered, "Limits?" He turned back, cocking his head quizzically. I tried not to sound like an idiot.

"Like...what? Can you give me a hint?" His smile became wider, uncannily resembling the expression that had been on the presenter's face...and on my husband's earlier. He didn't say anything, just shook his head and went about his business.

I sat down at a picnic table and looked at the blank sign, lost. How do you make up a sign stating your "limits" if you don't know what limits someone may think to push? How do you think of everything that may come up? You can't, I realized, and that was exactly what was so exciting and had my pussy throbbing just thinking about it.

Quickly I made the sign, before I could think about it much more, and turned it in to the organizers. They thanked me perfunctorily, told me to show up at 9:30, and that was that.

For them, at least. I was nervous as hell. I couldn't concentrate on anything as I waited for the minutes to crawl by. My husband sat with me on the stairs of the Objectification Room cabin, and I let all the "what ifs" come out of my brain.

"What if you can't handle it, honey? What if I can't? What if I freak out? But if I don't do it, what if I regret it forever?" He just smiled and listened, two things he was really good at. At my last "What if nobody wants to play with me?" he actually chuckled, and I joined him as I heard the insecure nine-year-old in my voice. We just rambled, and as the what-ifs came out, they lost power as we looked at each one together.

Suddenly it was 9:30, and time for me to go into the cabin. I had thought the room would be full of volunteers that I'd be lucky to get in at all, but it turned out I was the first one there, which meant I was in. Before I had time to really assimilate that, my sign of Do's and Don't's was hanging on the veil over Bed #3. The monitor explained everything to me as I sat on the edge of the bed waiting for the others to arrive. She was simply repeating what had been covered earlier, which was a good thing as I couldn't focus anyway. The butterflies in my stomach had become vultures and my breathing was shallow even as my pussy grew wetter and wetter. *This is really going to happen,* I thought suddenly, and felt my cunt spasm in response. I was going to be one of the naked naughty objects on a bed with no clue who was touching me.

The next "object" to arrive was a beautiful tanned girl who would be on the bed next to me. "I'm so nervous!" she confided to me as she sat down. "What if no one wants to play with me?"

I laughed at the thought that this pretty sexy thing was worried about the same thing I was. It helped put things into perspective. "Oh, honey," I chuckled at her. "You've got nothing to worry about." I tried to tell myself the same thing as two men arrived, and then finally another girl who would be in Bed #1. At the monitor's direction, we all stripped naked and lay down on the bed. The veils came down and hid the lower parts of our bodies from view.

The world suddenly seemed to shrink, in a beautiful way – our side of the veil was dimly lit by string lights along the ceiling and walls. It made the heavy cloth in front of our faces an exotic textured wall, dividing our reality from the other side, where I and four other people were naked and exposed. Totally vulnerable, and we couldn't see a thing. Suddenly we were all breathing hard, and I saw the others eyes begin to sparkle with excitement as our situation really began to sink in.

The What Ifs showed up again in force. What would happen to us? Would anyone show up at all? Would anyone be brave enough to use the objects? How would they want to use us…them? I stared at the ceiling, suddenly sure that the girl next to me would get all the attention, beautiful as she was. Suddenly I just hoped that somebody, anybody would play with me at all. *What if I just get left here, alone?* I thought, mortified at the humiliating possibility.

I heard someone check with our monitor, asking if the objects were ready to be used, and suddenly the butterflies were a full-force gale. I heard him walk outside the cabin, yelling to one and all "Attention, Campers, Pervs, and All Other Dirty-Minded Folk! The Objectification Room is open for business, with Objects available for Your Use! Come one, come all! "…if they're lucky!" came a distant voice, to the accompaniment of laughter. Then the sound cut off, and I realized they must have closed the door – I strained, but couldn't hear any footsteps. *That's it,* I thought, *no one's coming.* There was some wry amusement inside at the double entendre.

The monitor's voice on the other side of the veil suddenly passed across, telling someone about the rules of the room, the safety precautions…then there was silence again. The tan girl next to me gasped, and I realized someone was touching her. Straining my eyes, I could see a slight shadow through the fabric. They were playing with her. And she was enjoying it. Fingers touched my thigh, then, and I almost didn't believe it was real; the feeling was so dissociated at first. They pushed my thighs open, roughly playing with my lips, then sliding abruptly into my sopping wet cunthole. I almost laughed with joy and relief – I would have known that touch anywhere. I smiled as my husband played with me a while, then heard he distinct snapping sound of a latex glove being removed. I felt a little disappointed – I'd hoped he would show people just how slutty his slutwife could be. I loved how he made me feel, and suddenly the butterflies were gone, and I could just enjoy being an Object.

I turned my head to either side, looking at the faces of the others as they were played with. There came another touch on my legs, fabric this time, and I let out a moaning *mmmmmmm* at the sensuality of it. Just about the time I was getting curious about what they might have in mind, though, the touch was gone, and I sighed with disappointment. There was no more fear in me, though, nothing like the way I'd felt at first. I went back to watching the others get played with.

Wow, I thought, watching the tan girl get ridden by some unseen cock. Ridden hard, it seemed, there must have been at least two guys working her over. The guy on the far end was on all fours, now, turned over, and I thought *Good idea. Practical.* I wasn't exactly sure what was being done to him, but I could hazard a few guesses. The guy next to him apparently had peaked under the veil one too many times, and the monitor removed him from the bed. The other girl in Bed #1 is being used so hard and fast she can't even catch her breath.

And me, I stared at the ceiling fan.

Until, there were fingers on me, light and questing. They spread my legs apart, brushing against my mound…I heard the squirt of lube and almost protested that I didn't *need* any, I may have been a bit bored but my pussy sure wasn't. I felt the fingers play for a bit as I moaned and twisted, trying to move my body to get more fingers involved. Instead, *poof,* they disappeared, and I was left to look again at tan girl.

She was being fucked so hard that the monitor on our side had to sit on the edge of her bed; it was lifting up like a see-saw from the weight of all the bodies on the other side. I just went back to staring at the ceiling fan. *This is it,* I decided, *I'm counting to 30.* If nobody touched me, then obviously I wasn't the right type to be considered a desirable object. I wondered if I should have left my skirt on, to cover my belly…

Tan girl finally reached a point where she was exhausted from being continually used, and she left. I felt mixed emotions at this, a little embarrassed by them. On the one hand, I was glad she'd had a good time – but I was also feeling a little selfish satisfaction that now people would have to settle for me, and give me a good time.

I made it to 28, my mind fuzzy and almost asleep, when I felt another touch. More lube, more fingers, spreading me open, fucking me…then the person climbed up on me, and I felt the fire starting. I couldn't remember if objects were allowed to make noise or not, but it didn't matter – I couldn't stop the sounds coming from my mouth. He was on me, spreading my thighs, and his breath and moans matched mine. When he slid his cock into my pulsing pussy I let out an "Oh, YES!!" and didn't care if it broke the "objectification" fantasy – I was being taken, and my mind was full of *Ride me, show them that you got the cream of the crop because you don't judge by looks!* Uncharitable, perhaps, but that was where my brain went as he pounded hard and fast, exploding inside of me. I moaned in satisfaction – this was exactly how I dreamed of being used! Not for my pleasure, but for theirs. I heard him pull off the condom and throw it in the trash, felt the wetness of the lube between my thighs, and realized I wanted more. I wanted to be used again and again.

As if in answer to my need, I felt more lube being added, fingers probing, stroking my clit, pinching my lips. They fucked me with one finger, then two, pushing deep and wiggling in a deliciously wicked way. It made me twist, trying to get more, and I caught a glimpse of the monitor above me, smiling as she watched the expression on my face.

I humped the anonymous hand, begged for more with my body and my moans. I could feel their legs brush mine, but had no idea who it was – not even if it was a man or a woman. The headfuck was amazing. Anyone could be watching, or no one. I had no clue, no control about what would happen next. I only knew that they were getting pleasure using me. They fucked me deeper with their fingers, slid their hand up and down my slit, spread the wetness around…I found myself hoping, wishing they would just climb on and fuck me like the last person, but they just kept using their fingers…and eventually I realized they were trying to make me cum. I didn't want to cum! As I lay there writhing and panting I just wanted to be used.

I felt the person lean their crotch into my knee, and could feel the distinct texture of lace – panties or a petticoat, but definitely lace…and a warm cock under it! There was a guy wearing panties with a rock-hard cock getting off playing with my pussy. He was rubbing off against me, and I pressed my knee up, feeling him play harder with my cunt. The monitor came over to ask if I needed a glass of water, and I almost screamed at her, shaking my head violently *No, don't interrupt me NOW!* I could feel my orgasm building, but I didn't want to cum. I did my best to hold it off as his fingers worked me over, inside, fucking me, and finally his determination won over. I relaxed control and let go, the orgasm shuddering through me, unwitnessed by him. It was an amazing feeling, and as I stopped shaking I heard again the now-familiar sound of an unseen glove, covered in my cunt juice, being snapped off his hands and thrown in the trash.

Before I could catch my breath, there were more hands at my cunt, fingering me, again trying to drive me to orgasm. I knew there was no way I would cum like that again, even as they made me moan loudly with the pleasure they were giving me. At the same time, I started to think that my time in the Objectification Room was about done…once I cum, I'm usually done. I decided to give it just a little longer, as the unknown hands leave.

There's a pause then, a bit of a breather, and I was just about to signal the monitor that I was ready to go, when I heard a male voice from the other side of the veil. "Ah…this one looks like it would be fun to play with. Mmm, look at that cunt!" I felt rough hands grab my thighs, spreading my legs wide apart. Fingers plunged into me, rough the way I like it, not playing like the last one. These fingers simply took what they wanted, and when they pulled out, I heard the man's satisfaction at what he found.

"Ah, wet and juicy like a good cunt should be."

I heard a girlish whisper, then, and the man says "Kneel down, girl, and see for yourself." I heard movement, and then there were tiny hands, tentative, reaching into my pussy. I moved my leg to give her better access, and the man laughed. "Oh, it's ready, alright. What a slut it must be. You could take a lesson from this one, pet." His strong hands grabbed my leg, lifting it higher, as she poked and prodded. "Girl, it's got a nice big pussy. You can use more than one finger, I suspect." I felt the girl use two fingers, then three, twisting and turning them as she gained confidence, and in spite of my earlier orgasm I felt the fire begin to burn again deep inside.

When she pulled her hand out, I spread my legs wide in desperation. *Don't tell me she's done?!?* My body begged her, willing for more. "Fold your fingers…into a cone, like this," I heard him say, and I realized he was going to have her fist me. Their voices faded to urgent whispers, but I was able to pick out words here and there, possibly because all of my senses were focused on the other side of the veil. Her fingers finally came back to my pussy, but before she could push them in, I felt his hand brush hers aside and grab my cunt brutally. "I bet you like it rough, don't you?" he demanded.

I couldn't help the keening, pleading "Yesssssss…" that escaped my lips, past the thin fabric that separated us.

"Ah, it has a voice!" he snickered, with a pleased tone in his voice. I found a strange satisfaction that I had given him pleasure even in this small way.

The girl came back to my pussy, sliding one finger, two, three, then a fourth, her small hand finally starting to fill me the way I wanted. I felt her thumb slide in, then, and electricity shot through my body, clit to nipples.

Then she seemed to figure it out, and she fisted me hard. I wanted to cum for her, as I rode her fist, sweating and moaning and begging incoherently for *more, harder, deeper.* The girl gave me all she could, and bless her; she brought me close to the edge, where I teetered for a glorious, frustrating time. She pounded and pinched my clit with her other hand, while her master kept whispering to her about this object she was playing with. I can hear the hoarse arousal in his voice even when I don't hear all the words...

Finally, his voice rises. "Time to move on, pet." I suddenly found tears in my eyes – I was crying. Again came the snap of the glove, the sound of it being discarded, and I heard them move on. Shaking, I pulled my legs from under the barrier and sit up. I wondered, just for a second, if I should stay longer...but no. I knew it was time to find my husband. Still trembling, I got dressed, and thanked the monitor when she brought me a cup of water.

From the other side of the veil came a voice. "Awww... what happened to Object #3?" For just an instant I wanted to strip down again, to slide back under, but another part knew I was worn out, well-used, and wanted to spend the rest of the evening with my husband.

I found him easily, and we decided to try something more cooperative. As we entered the Orgy Room, he walked me around until he found an unoccupied mattress, where he bent me over with my ass in the air. Just before his hard cock plunges into me – his, my husband's, the one I know better than any other, slamming into me so beautifully – I hear him say, proudly, "My slut...my beautiful slut."

I am his.

WALKING THROUGH FEARS

dawn says

As you may have noticed, many of these stories involved walking through a fear of one sort or another. Whether the story is one based on reality, or one based on fantasy; they are situations that make us look in the mirror at our slutty selves. This can be a scary place. Many of us, especially girls, were taught that 'good girls' don't do this. But, deep down, we are sexual beings with creative imaginations. We have stories in our heads that we want to act upon. We may want to be the slut that is gang-banged, or we want to be the one that helps a slut fulfill their fantasy, thereby embracing our sluthood as well.

All I know is that i wanted to be free enough to try these fantasies that I had dreamt about for so long. Damn being a 'good girl'; i wanted to experience life through my sexual self. To do that though, i had to overcome one of the biggest hurdles: fear.

If you allow fear to control your actions, what will we ever experience? Some fear is valid of course, it is our way of protecting ourselves. It is a reaction that could keep us alive in certain circumstances. But, with the stories you have read or will read after this, there wasn't anything in there that would have harmed me. We looked out for our safety, we used safer sex methods, we had safe calls in place, we made sure to be in environments that we could control for the most part, and then we took a breath and jumped in with both feet.

Of the stories in this book, were you able to pick out fantasy from reality? i'm sure a couple might have stood out as one or the other, but some may have you guessing. i will give you a hint, there are more that are reality based than fantasy based. We have walked forward, bringing our fantasies to life.

Because of that we now have stories to tell when we are sitting in a rocker in our old age, wonderful stories. Will your reflective stories begin with 'remember when' or 'I wish I had of'?

WITCH HUNT

It all started on a Thursday, or was it earlier in the week than that? I'm not sure. I do remember that I was parked in front of my Master's work building. It was cold outside but I had the heat cranking in my truck and was listening to our local rock station on the radio. I had brought Master dinner as I was apt to do when he was working second shift. It was a service that I enjoyed being able to do for him; a nice hot dinner on a cold day. I looked up from the book I was reading and spotted him heading my way, from the front door of the building. I excitedly hit the button that dropped the window; sucking in my breath as the cold hit my face, but with a big smile on my face. The sight of him always gives me a little thrill.

Well, he usually gives me a kiss and a 'thank you' when I hand him his dinner, but this time I almost dropped his dinner as he grabs my hair and growls into my ear. My smile quickly disappeared and concern filled my body. At first, I really thought I had done something wrong. My heart started racing and I couldn't breathe. Instead of berating me though, he growls into my ear, "Our scene for Friday night starts now. You are not to join the attendees-only mailing list and you are to find me a bag about the size of a backpack; no questions. Understood?"

The butterflies start deep in the pit of my stomach as my thighs began to feel the wetness of my pussy, just from having my hair grabbed. "Yes Sir." My fear of having displeased him, instantly takes a turn to delight and a different kind of fear.

I look into his eyes, seeing the seriousness and the twinkle. I feel a little smile cross my lips as I realize that he has created something that will culminate in a surprise. My eyes take on a twinkle of their own. Yet, despite the excitement, or maybe because of it, the butterflies continue to grow in size.

He lets go of my hair, looks me in the eye, takes his dinner from my motionless hands and strides away with a purposeful gate. *Did I see a hurriedly hidden smirk?* I slowly roll up the window. *What could he possibly have in mind? That smirk doesn't bode well for me; or does it?* We've been together for so long that scenes like this rarely happen.

This has totally taken me by surprise but I can feel the results of it throughout my body. The glazed eyes, the slow to respond limbs as I attempt to start the truck, the juiciness between my thighs; even my nipples are standing on end. He has tapped into my submissiveness and sluttiness, as only he can. Yet, the only thought in my head was that I needed to find a bag the size of a backpack.

I think about the possibilities all the way home. My mind takes turns with racing with ideas and slowing down to a crawl as I realize that trying to figure out his mind is fruitless. I would have hated being the person driving behind me as my speed matched the pace of my thoughts.

The thoughts continued: *what did he have in mind? What would have him thinking this far ahead for a scene?* Over time we had become more intuitive with our play at events and in our personal space; not putting anything together until we found a piece of equipment to play on and figured out what toys we had brought, if any. Sometimes, we wouldn't need a piece of equipment and would just play in the middle of the dungeon or on our bed.

My mind continued to race. I barely remember driving home at all. It's all a blur of thoughts. *A bag; why would he need a bag? Did it matter what color? What size of backpack? What was he going to put into it? What did he have in mind? And why couldn't I join the attendees list for the event that was happening that weekend? What was he keeping secret? Would others be able to keep it a secret?* I certainly didn't want to join the list and spoil the surprise, *but why talk about our scene on a public list? What could it be?* My mind was racing with all the possibilities and through it all I found myself erotically turned on.

I waited at home, all excited, hoping he would have more clues for me when he got home from work. But, none were forthcoming as he walked in the door and then settled down for a good night's sleep, a slight smile on his lips.

The next day began with scene ideas being thought of and discarded. We were sitting next to each other, working on computer projects as was our pattern during the day before he went to work. The dog was sleeping at my feet, the cat on his lap, light music playing in the background. Then, something in my thoughts had me speak without thinking first; asking a question about the scene. I don't remember what the mindless question was, but his reaction was instant. He jumped up from his computer chair, quickly pulled his t-shirt off over his head, came to me and wrapped it around my throat, growling to me that I shouldn't worry about anything to do with the scene: that he had 17 volunteers to help him and it wasn't for me to worry about, it was all under control.

He quickly released the shirt and went back to his desk as if nothing had happened. I sat there, stunned and having to concentrate on my breathing once he released the shirt; feeling the pressure of it still on my throat, though it was gone. I was so excited;

hyperventilating at this point was a definite possibility. I had to concentrate, *breathe in, breathe out*. The sound of me sucking in air was loud in the room, over the clicks of his keyboard and the music in the background. He looked at me with a sparkle in his eye, excited by all of this as much as I was, though trying not to show it. The idea of how this was turning him on, turned me on, which made the situation even more erotic and powerful.

The instant faded and we slowly went back to our normal day; though I know each of us were thinking about what was coming up on Friday in our own way. I don't know about Master, but I was wet and having problems breathing normally all day long. The excitement was causing butterflies and memory issues. He would have to ask me twice to get something for him, which is very unlike me. Though, he knew why I was behaving the way I was, and it became part of the scene as well; each of us playing with the energy and emotions this was creating.

We go through the pattern of Master leaving for work and coming home again afterwards. I'm sure there was some flirting and baiting going on through the evening as we stayed in contact, but it was the words of the following morning that had me all a jitter.

That following morning, Thursday, he wakes me up and whispers into my ear that he will be releasing 'Thing' during our scene. *'Thing'? Really?* The hyperventilating starts again. I think about 'Thing' and the possibilities. You see...'Thing' is his primal side; his beast within. 'Thing' rarely makes an appearance when we scene because Sir has such a tight grip on him. But, when he does appear, it's deep and dark; our scenes turn into intense shows of power, with 'thing' completely taking me owning me, no matter what it takes. Master's words stay with me through the day, coloring everything I do or think about. The idea scared me, which excited me, which made me wet and then the cycle would start over again.

At this point, I'm beyond curious. But, I've run all the possible scenes I can think of through my head and it's not matching some of the stuff he is telling me. There is just enough information to scare and intrigue me, but not enough for me to figure anything out. But, I know enough and I know enough about him to know that this has the possibility of being over the edge of intense. He is so creative that it really could be anything. So, I decide to stop thinking about the details of the scene and just enjoy the emotions and feelings that are currently running through my sensitive, reactive body.

Friday can't get here fast enough, but of course, it finally arrives. My job is to pack the toy bag and the suitcase. But, there is one item that he packs himself; the backpack that he demanded I buy for him. We pack, while thoughts continue to race through my head. We load the car, but he is careful not to let me pick up the special bag, toying with me as me makes sure that I see him put the bag in the trunk.

We drive to the event; on pins and needles, knowing I can't ask all the questions I want to ask. He's not talking about the scene this day. Except for the bag, nothing else happened or was said that gave any hint that a scene was going to happen at all. Was it all to get me worked up? But nothing was really going to happen? Maybe that's what it is. I breathe a sigh of relief and disappointment in a single breath, feeling let down but knowing that I wouldn't hold it against him if that is all it had been. The emotions I had run through and the excitement was well worth it.

We get to the hotel, get checked in, unload our stuff in the hotel room, including the backpack that has stuff in it; of what, I know not. He then asks for my collar. This is a ritual for us that is very important. I close my eyes, forgetting about everything else and the confusion that I'm feeling. I open my eyes a little and see that his are closed as well as we both become mindful of the moment. I feel his finger on my throat and then the weight of the leather collar as he presses it against my skin. I reach up, pulling my hair out of the way as he locks the collar at the nape of my neck. We both take a breath, he takes my hand and out the door we go.

The oddness begins as soon as we arrive downstairs; people coming up to us and making quick comments, and then walking away. It's kind of like a drive by harassing. I'm not sure how to handle it. I look at Master. He just looks back at me as if nothing is going on, but watches my reaction.

'You are in trouble,' says one of them menacingly, looking me straight in the eye.

'I hear you've been bad,' says another with a smile, which she is quick to hide as she disappears.

This happens more than a few times. At first, it confuses and scares me. I have no clue what to make of it. Have I been bad and Master is going to punish me in front of everyone? My heart begins to race and real fear sets in. I look Master for his reaction but see none. After a couple of deep breaths, reason begins to set in. *I haven't been bad. Sir wouldn't do a punishment scene if I hadn't done something to deserve it. And to punish me in front of so many people that we know? What would the punishment be? I would have to have done something totally unforgivable to be punished in that manner; something on the level of having my collar removed. But, I can't think of anything I've done, small or large, to deserve such treatment.* So, now that I've gotten rid of the worst possible scenario, I can calm down enough to wonder what is really going on. I take a deep breath, trying not to let the fear show, knowing I'm not doing a great job at it. I look at Master. He has a sparkle in his eye again and a smirk on his lips. He knows this is driving me crazy. He knows how my mind works and has probably heard all the questions in my head, but I'm hanging in there without asking them out loud, a look of fear and confusion on my face.

After some more drive-by harassment, the evening of play begins. It's noisy and there are a lot of people crammed into the dungeon and social area. Master dismisses me, telling me to go and socialize and that our scene is at 10:45. Wow, it's even got a starting time to it. Now I'm really not sure what is going on and I'm getting a little nervous. This could be anything. Trying to repress my nervousness, I go to socialize with our friends. It becomes a little difficult though to make small talk, as there is an undercurrent with those that I'm talking with.

Master has told me to come look for him at 10:30pm. Because of another responsibility he needed to take care of earlier, I am not to look for him until 10:30pm. I watch the clock with excitement and, what is that feeling, trepidation? I socialize for the time being, trying to be pleasant and attentive to those I'm interacting with, but I find my thoughts racing, my mouth dry, my hands shaking; the sounds of whips and moans from the dungeon barely making it past the fog in my head. I haven't felt this nervous in a very long time and the butterflies in my stomach are having a battle.

At 10:30 on the nose, I excuse myself and go off to find him. He is ready and has been searching for me as well. We find each other easily, showing how excited we both are at the prospect in front of us. I see that he has the backpack as he guides me into the dungeon. Hand in hand, we walk around in the huge, dimly lit room, thumpy base music filling the air; full of people in various states of undress, participating in or watching all that is taking place in the room. After a while, he chooses a table near the middle of the dungeon, but slight to the side. This is a little unusual to me, as we usually look for a piece of furniture that is hidden away from others. This is more visible which certainly plays to my exhibitionist side.

We stand next to the table, just staring at each other. I pay attention, keenly aware, so that I can follow his lead. I don't know what to expect. He takes a breath, blocking out the noises and action in the room and focuses on me. He looks me in the eye as we breathe together; in, out, in, out, slower, in out. My eyes start to feel heavy and I relax somewhat. I find that I'm not worried about what is going to happen. I trust him completely. All the stories and confusion lay at my feet as I become mindful of the moment and the experience itself. The dungeon noises become background to our breathing.

He leans in and helps me to undress, breath on my shoulders, hands sliding off my dress, stroking my hyper-sensitive skin. His breath moves to my neck and I feel my knees go soft as I almost melt to the floor. Instead, I arch in with a moan. His touch, breath and focused energy drive me wild and any walls that may have been in place have totally crashed at this point. As the last item of clothing rests in his hands, I feel totally naked and vulnerable. In the back of my head I am aware of the energy of people watching.

He gently takes off my glasses and lays them on a small table beside him. With his hot touch, he takes me by the shoulders and turns me around to face the far end of the room. 'See that cross beam over there?" he asks me. I nod my head yes, not understanding, but seeing the beam he is referring to. I have enough thought process left to wonder why he is asking me this; my understanding was that we'd be playing on the table behind us. "Do you think you could walk fast to it without your glasses?' Confused, I turn to look at him while answering, 'Yes Sir,' knowing that I could.

Satisfied with my answer, he turns to the table and covers it with a fur that we bring specifically for me to lay on. With a firm hand he helps me climb up onto the table, my fur, directing me to lie on my back. With a gentle, caressing touch, he puts on my blindfold. My head has begun to spin out of its calmness as the darkness descends. *Why ask me a question like that and then put me on the table?*

I know to wait, to let it go. *But why would he do that? Breathe. Enjoy the moment. It might play in what he has planned. It might be to scare me. It might be to throw me off of his real plan; whatever it is, he doing a great job at twisting my head so that I can't guess. He may even have changed his mind from the original plan. This has happened before. So, I've learned not to second guess him. But, why would I need to walk fast? What does that have to do with now? Relax. Enjoy. Don't overthink.*

As if he can't hear the silent questions in my head, he slowly starts warming me up; rubbing warmth into my skin, flogging me sensually. The thoughts melt away as I begin to float towards subspace. My body loves sensual touch and is enjoying every moment of this. Soft, sensual, naughty brushes against my nipples and thighs have me moaning and squirming under his touch. He leans down, breathing on my neck. I feel like I'm going to have a body orgasm just from this additional touch of air, as my back arches and I shiver all over.

But instead of helping me fly over the edge, he leans in with his lips touching my ear, whispering, "lot of prep work for such a small scene, wasn't it?' I just smile, knowing that this has been exceptionally beautiful, and if all that build up was going to end with a scene of this nature, I was perfectly content and happy with such; though, not wanting it to stop. *Wait.* My head wakes up a little. *Why is he talking to me?* He rarely talks during a scene unless it's naughty talk.

It comes to be that my head was right to have a question. I feel Master get off the table and touch my hand. Holding onto my hand, he slowly pulls me to a sitting position and guides me off the table. Not unusual. This wouldn't be the first time he has shifted positions with me during the scene. The energy in the room starts to change. The music and other scenes are starting to come into focus as Master holds my hand, standing next to the table. He's not moving. He's not changing my position. It feels like he is waiting for something.

He reaches behind me and pulls the blindfold slowly off my head. The sound of the room has come into focus, but my sight and awareness of what is going on has not. He steps back from me. I feel a little shaky without his support, not having a clue as to what is going on. *Are we done? Should I be looking for my clothes?* Something feels unfinished, incomplete. It's not like him to end a scene like this. I feel disappointment rise and then swallow it, knowing what we just did was beautiful and if that was it, that was it.

I look at the floor, trying not to show my disappointment, wondering where he has put my clothes. At this point, he puts a finger under my chin, lifting it and looking at me intently. In a deep, steady voice he says, "If I was you, I would run." I look at him with confusion. My head is trying to switch gears. *Run?* I look at him for confirmation that I heard correctly, feeling unsteady on my feet. He keeps eye contact with me, a few inches from my face and says again, 'If I were you, I would run!" in that deep commanding voice and points toward the other end of the dungeon.

He steps back and then pointing at me, he yells, "A witch!!!"

It hits me: it's a witch hunt! I forget his words of 'walk fast', and take off running.

They are not going to catch me! I hear the chant of random voices throughout the dungeon along with Master's. 'A witch, a witch!!!' I dodge and run, but suddenly people part and I'm given a path to run through. I don't get very far though before the people close back in and I see people trying to stop me. But, I'm not going to let them. I dodge and make sharp turns around and away from people trying to get me. All I hear is the blood pounding through my ears and his voice saying something about the beam across the cavernous room. Focusing on the goal of the beam, I pull from people's hands. I don't have on any clothes, running naked, so they don't have much to grab onto. I feel hands on my arms and legs. I hear people panting as they try to pull me down. 'Get her. Don't let her get away. Come on, she can't be that hard to catch. Stop the witch!!!' But, they can't keep a hold on me. The adrenaline and fear have taken control of my body and they are having difficulty slowing me down. Then, out of nowhere, someone grabs me and throws me down to the floor. I'm amazed that they didn't hurt me and in a flash realized that I enjoyed it. I close my eyes as I see people grab for me, holding me down. I struggle, but I'm not really scared. I figured it had to be Master. He's the only one that has been able to throw me down like that. But, then I realize it doesn't feel like Master and I don't hear his voice. People are grabbing me and holding me down. I'm kicking and growling. I can't get away. I still don't hear Master's voice giving direction. I don't know why, but I keep my eyes closed, not wanting to see who is grabbing me. I don't like that I can't hear his voice.

Then, without any warning, my head and emotions switch to darkness and all I can think about is that these people have no right to be hitting me and holding me down. *Who the hell do they think they are?* I take a look around. My glasses are off and the adrenaline is pumping, so I'm not able to focus very well. *Where is Master, my protector?* I see a few people that I recognize and they are smiling as they are holding me down and beating me. Somehow, instantly, even though I'm in the land of fear and still kicking, yelling, growing; it feels safe. A little voice in my head tells me to just go along with this, play with the fear and the anger and let it all out. These people are having fun with this and I'm not in a position where I can hurt anyone. They are doing a good job of watching out for my kicking and biting. I always wondered if I could do resistance play, now is my chance. Of course this was all thought in a flash. I was zoning and angry, but now layering in some fun as well, which made it even more intense.

A couple of times they had me pinned down so completely that I couldn't move. I almost gave up at that time. But, then someone would shift and it would give me an opportunity to twist away. I'd be back on my knees trying to crawl away. Then, I'd be down again and screaming in rage at being trapped. My beast was out in all her glory and those playing with me loved it. I could feel the carpet against my skin, hear the panting of those involved, feel the grips on my ankles and wrists. Someone was spanking me with a paddle as I was held still. Someone else was twisting a nipple, daring me to pull away and then laughing when I tried.

In the excitement of noise, I could hear a couple of people yelling at me to repent. Then I would hear a whisper in my ear that everything was ok. That helped remind me of where I was and I could refocus on the fun/fear aspect.

At one point, someone grabbed my feet and started tickling. Oh hell. That's a hard limit I forget to tell people about. I couldn't help it. The rage took control. I had to get away. My beast came out in full force. At one point, I opened my eyes and saw the person tickling me with a smile on their face. It struck me that they were doing this to make my scene more intense. It was an instant recognition that most of these people were doing it because they loved me and though they were having a good time, they wanted me to have a good time as well. I closed my eyes and continued to fight, giving them what we all wanted; relishing the fact that I could just be naked and vulnerable in a crowd of people that loved me.

Then, during a single breath, everyone let go for a second. I had no time to question why. I took that opportunity to get on my feet and try running again. Instead I was caught by at least 2 people and while standing, I was held tight from behind. I struggled but was held firm against someone's chest. I 'felt' who it was and settled down a little; feeling safe, but still tried to get away.

It was at that point that everything stopped. Though I was held tight, people weren't touching me or yelling at me. There was still noise in the dungeon, but not from our group. I could feel the stillness. All I could hear was breathing. I knew everyone was still there, because the energy was crackling around us, but nothing was happening. My eyes were still closed so that I could feel the energy of what was taking place. I came to an understanding that the next step was mine; everyone was waiting on me. I took a gulp of air, and opened my eyes. Instant fear overcame me: a couple of inches from my face, staring at me intently, was a blacker than black face and bright white eyes. Master was here. Master was a demon. 'Mine,' he growls and I'm let go from the person whose arms kept me from falling down. 'To the table,' he commands. Two from the group walk me silently across the room, naked, panting. They leave me at the table, smiles reaching their eyes, seeming to express, 'lucky girl'. Master/Demon takes my arm, pushing me roughly back up onto the original table, belly to fur.

The crying begins as my cheek touches the fur. The intensity is overwhelming. But, he has just begun. With a growl, he climbs on the table, onto my back and rakes his fingernails down my flesh. It feels like he is slicing me open. I arch and cry harder, knowing it's 'Thing' on my back, holding me down and taking me, marking me as His. I welcome him completely, body, mind and soul. Knowing he won't harm me, knowing more pain is to come; mind-blowing, blissful, transforming pain.

He pulls back onto his haunches and the punching begins; deep, bruising punches to my hips and ass. He growls and yells in his own language as he continues to pound my flesh, taking what he wants, over and over, deeper and deeper. The intensity has me flying high. Everything in the room has disappeared. All I can hear and feel is us making music in our own special way.

I feel his prod to flip over. I do so, daring to take a peek at him; seeing the darkness, seeing the glowing eyes, seeing the realness. We have both become vulnerable to the other for this scene; walls down, souls open. He punches my breasts, my hips. Roughly, he spreads my thighs and punches my mound and pussy. With wild abandon, I grind back into his fist, responding with need, hungry for more. He smacks my nipples, bringing the intense pain I'm begging for.

He prods me to flip again and climbs on top of me once more; scratching, biting, growling in my ear. I can't stop crying in profound release.

Another flip. More punching between my thighs; pinching of my clit and lips, slapping of the nipples, passionate growling, intense taking.

Once he has taken all that is his, he begins to slow down. My breathing slows down as I realize he is putting 'Thing' away. The energy shifts. Quietly, gently, he helps me sit up and wraps me in his arms and lets me cry. It's so beautiful. Softly, he helps me down from the table, wrapping me in my fur.

A friend that helped with the scene brings us some very much needed water. My throat is raw from all the yelling and crying. I'm a shivering mess at this point as he leads me over to the chairs. Master asks another friend to sit with me for a moment as he cleans up our play area so that someone else can play.

There was a lot of snuggling aftercare after that; kisses and hair stroking, deep love and connection.

AFTERCARE

dawn says

Aftercare may be a concept you've heard of, maybe not. It's the care that we give to each other after a scene; after opening ourselves up and becoming vulnerable to our lover and our inner selves. In the intensity of the moment, being slutty is easier than when we come down from the endorphins that may have been generated by the experience. Scening or having intense sex, or fulfilling a fantasy can have us flying high and to keep from crashing to the ground, we need to be proactive and create a safety net of sorts. This safety net is referred to as 'after care'.

After participating in a BDSM scene, many bottoms will enter into a state called 'sub-space'. This is where the endorphins have kicked in either from pain or from becoming vulnerable to physical sensations or intense emotions. Some people may refer to this as trancing; some may refer to it as floating. Either way, it should be acknowledged and taken care off. Aftercare is the proactive step in heading off 'sub-drop'. This is when the endorphins that cause you to fly, get absorbed back into your body and you can go through a chemical crash. This can cause a short period of depression. We don't want that to happen, so we do our best to remember and provide aftercare.

For the most part aftercare may be handled in a physical way; cuddling in a blanket, drinking water, and maybe even eating chocolate. This is to help our bodies to recover from something so intense; physically and emotionally. It may be directed by the person that topped the bottom during a scene, or it may have been negotiated to where it's not the top, but someone else that will perform the aftercare of the bottom. Either way, I can't overstate the importance of this final step of a scene, especially if sub-space was entered into.

But there is another type of aftercare we need to be aware of as well. With 'slutty sex' there will be moments that physical aftercare should be done, but there is also a psychological aftercare that needs to come into play. Slutty sex, as described in some of these stories, has the potential to scare us. For me, I needed to know that my partner still loved me, still cherished me. I was ok with being seen as 'slutty', but didn't want him to think that I was 'too slutty'. There is a line, though I'm not exactly sure what that line is. All I know is that I needed his reassurance that we were walking this path together.

So, for us, after a scene where we've involved slutty sex or sensual humiliation, we make sure to talk about it later over a bowl of cereal or go grocery shopping. We go on with our normal lives. This is to give us confidence that everything is ok.

One day I really needed to know that everything was ok. I asked Dan, 'was that too slutty'; he looked me directly in the eyes and said, "of course not, who do you think is on this journey with you? If you are too slutty, than so am I." That's all I needed to hear.

This fear of rejection or abandonment could last for a couple of days. This type of aftercare involves reassuring them that all is good and it was an exciting experience.

ALL GOOD THINGS

Dan says

Writing an ending to this book has been a tricky task for us, because we have to ask "what do I hope you, the reader, got from this?" We hope you learned from our mistakes and missteps, and we hope you got something from the concepts we shared.

We hope the stories gave you ideas, and we hoped they turned you on. We'd be very complimented to hear you self-pleasured to our adventures.

We hope you had fun guessing "Did they really do this?" or "I can't picture them really doing that" and we hope you got it right – and sometimes wrong.

But the most important thing is we hope you read this and said "I am allowed". Because you are – you are allowed to be as slutty, authentic, naughty, and wild as you want to be. Though, we hope the parts on being ethical about it also stuck as well.

Remember – There will be a day when it is past the time of doing and instead time to reflect. We hope between now and then you will write some stories of your own.

dawn says

Most of us growing up were told that 'good girls' and 'good boys' don't behave like this. i'm here to tell you that 'oh yes we do' and we are enjoying ourselves in the process.

i'm also assuming that you'd like to know if you guessed right on the stories. Remember, there are 6 that we have done, and 4 that are fantasies that have not been played through…yet.

Hotel Spanking, yes. Beach Bar, no. Grouse Flogging, yes. Shower, no. Susie's Reward, yes. Wench, though the dinner was based on a true story, no to the rest. Aphrodite's Temple, yes. Hard Paddled, no. Objectification Room, yes. Witch Hunt, yes.

How close did you get? Never-the-less, we hope you enjoyed.

BACKGROUND

About the Authors

Dan and dawn, a married couple for a number of years, found a way to co-create a relationship that at first they thought only fantasy. During their lifetimes, both before their relationship and during, they have experienced many lessons and fascinating discoveries that they like to share with others, especially in the alternative communities. Fortunately, opportunity has provided them various avenues to share these stories and experiences to any willing to listen.

Some of these avenues include; facilitating workshops, presentations, roundtable discussions, and intensives throughout North America, on various subjects from BDSM, M/s, Spirituality, Sacred Sexuality, Swinging, Polyamory, and other alternative sexualities. Their topics can range from Finding Your Authentic Self, Slutty Sex for Real Relationships, to Sensual Spanking.

Along with presenting, Dan and dawn also record and air a weekly internet radio show (podcast) called **Erotic Awakening**. Erotic Awakening focuses on many naughty topics (as well as other topics of interest) to their ever growing listener base of both people new to the slutty lifestyle as well as those more experienced.

They are also authors of the book, '**Living M/s**', **GLLA Master/slave 2010 titleholders**, leaders of the leather tribe '**House Metta**', creators of the sacred sexuality training program, '**Path of the Qadishti**', and facilitators of the sacred touch space '**Scarlet Sanctuary**'.

When they are not traveling for their various projects, Dan is employed as an IT technician in a Fortune 100 company and dawn tries to keep their projects organized as well as being a licensed clergy, full-time student and housewife. They live in Central Ohio with a various number cats and the occasional grandchild underfoot.

LIVING M/s

A Book for Masters, slaves, and Their Relationships

Dan and Dawn Williams

Foreword by Robert J. Rubel, PhD